and Other Tales of Christian Life

Bob Reed

PEAKE ROAD
Macon, Georgia

ISBN 1-57312-041-3

The Potluck Dinner That Went Astray
and
Other Tales of Christian Life

Bob Reed

Copyright © 1996
Peake Road

6316 Peake Road
Macon, Georgia 31210-3960
1-800-747-3016

Peake Road
is an imprint of
Smyth & Helwys Publishing, Inc.®

All rights reserved.
Printed in the United States of America.

The paper used in this publication meets the minimum
requirements of American Standard for Information
Sciences—Permanence of Paper for Printed Library Material.
ANSI Z39.48–1984.

Library of Congress #95-48117

Contents

Preface v

The Potluck Dinner that Went Astray 1

Aunt Ethel forgets to assign each housewife a specific dish to bring to a potluck dinner, thus creating a disaster and prompting the Methodists to develop a rule for all future potlucks.

The Tall Tale of the Little Church that Could 9

A country church survives for more than 165 years due to Baptist optimism, Congregational self-determination, Greek inspiration, and the Yankee eccentricities of Clyde the sexton.

The Praying Pigs 23

An African Methodist Episcopal farmer teaches his pigs how to pray, prompting the Presbyterians and other mainstream denominations to informally ban all individual praying out loud in their churches.

Doing the Right Thing for the Wrong Reasons 32

The political actions of two scoundrels inadvertently bring together the Methodists and Catholics in a little town, changing its character forever.

The Potluck Dinner that Went Astray

Washed in the Blood of the Lamb 45

> *The Baptists and Presbyterians quietly compete for members with the Calvinists, temporarily winning because of their inaction, thus setting an example for other denominations.*

Cousin Emma and the Great Bicycle Rebellion 55

> *Spurred on by a feisty woman, the Methodist church reluctantly becomes involved in social change and the temperance and women's suffrage movements.*

Funny, He Doesn't Look Presbyterian 76

> *After considerable anguish, a white suburban Presbyterian church hires a black minister.*

About the Author 90

Preface

The pages that follow offer a funny look at some of the follies and foibles of various people from mainstream Christian denominations. The seven stories seek to elevate those souls to a natural state of grace through adventures and misadventures.

Most of the folk are swept along in events because of the tyranny of small decisions. One thing leads to another, and before they know it they are carried away on a voyage that ends in a little moral or lesson.

This book is a work of fiction. Needless to say, names, incidents, characters, and places are either the product of the author's imagination or are used fictitiously. Any resemblance to actual persons living or dead is purely coincidental.

The stories are based on the premise that God has a sense of humor. It is said that God made us in His own image, and so far as we know, we are the only creatures to possess the gift of laughter.

While the tales tweak some Christian traditions and practices, I hope they might wake us up with a little pinch, by humorously reminding us how mysterious and wonderful life is when the fates and God take a hand.

A few stalwart souls looked at some of the stories in this collection and offered thoughts and comments or suggested corrections or deletions. They also offered much encouragement. Among them were Rick and Mary Ellen Breitenfeld, Bette and Charlie Carcano, Bill Harper, Phyllis and Dean Peterson, Chuck and Leonora Marquis, Barbara Roper, and the Reverends David Harvey and Sam Lee. Some others contributed occasional remarks, but they wish to remain anonymous, because their mothers tried desperately not to raise foolish children.

For Max and her patience and love

The Potluck Dinner that Went Astray

When you become a member of a Christian church, you're bound to hear about the "Lutheran Potluck Rule." It's also referred to by many as "The Four W's Rule." And it's sometimes just called "The Rule" for short.

Under whatever name, the informal ordinance has been in existence for more than fifty years, and it's a pretty good thing to adhere to if you are a woman and are put in charge of a church dinner—and you will be. Every adult female member of a mainstream denomination draws that duty at some time. The rule is also useful for any nonreligious gathering where people contribute individual dishes for everyone to consume.

They say the unofficial regulation stems from a disastrous incident that happened during World War II in a small midwestern town. It was sort of a potluck dinner that went astray.

It seems that a boy named Billy was to be welcomed home. He had been given an unexpected shore leave while his ship was being repaired at Puget Sound, but he only had seven days leave. What with train delays and all in the journey to and from the West Coast to Iowa, it appeared that he would be home for less than three days.

So for him to see all of his relatives and friends, something had to be organized. There were many willing hands, because some 53 souls in the small town of 357 residents were related to him in one way or another.

It wasn't that he was so special, but he was one of the youngest local boys to serve—he had seen action in the South Pacific—and he was a rather shy, stringbean kind of a lad with a sort of loopy grin who was liked by everybody.

Well, the whole thing kinda' got out of hand. More and more people wanted to see Billy, and the gathering that was originally planned as a Sunday afternoon relative drop-in at Uncle Dave's somehow got turned into a whole-town potluck picnic at the city park, across from the Emmanuel Lutheran Church.

Cousin George, who was the janitor of the church, was to take care of the folding chairs and tables, because the park's two picnic tables wouldn't handle the expected crowd. The Luther League kids would help set them up. Billy's mother said she'd bring the paper tablecloths

The Potluck Dinner that Went Astray

and napkins and the red, white, and blue crepe paper for the table decorations. And Minnie and Violet Guttenkoff, who were Billy's third cousins once removed, said they'd make the drinks of Kool Aid and iced tea.

That left the food to Aunt Ethel, whose idea the whole thing was. She was the head of the Lutheran Church Women (LCW) and was also sort of in charge of any civic functions in town. She liked "helping out with her organizational talents," as she rather primly put it.

Ethel was the only daughter of the town's physician, "Doc" Nelson. He was dead now, but as the only medical practitioner within thirty miles for many years, he had been a significant force in the area.

He had established his practice around the turn of the century and for a few years made his rounds in a horse and buggy. But he had been the first person in the county to buy an automobile and install a telephone. It connected his home with his examining rooms and was a marvel of modernity, folks said. Doc graduated to Model T's, and as other people got phones and cars, his life had become easier and his practice more efficient.

He was much beloved and respected. Nearly everybody in the area had doctored with him, and most had owed him money at one time or another.

Doc had been the only one in town to make any money during the Depression, and faced with a surplus of funds, he had plowed them back into the town. He ended up owning more than a third of Main Street and had started his two sons off in business, one as the president of the bank and the other as the owner of the lumber yard. His success and money had attracted a number of his wife's relatives, and he had been instrumental in staking them to business enterprises that served a wider clientele than the citizens in the little town.

Among those who flocked to his protective wing were his wife's cousin, "Digby" Darnell, who had established the undertaking parlor. A few folk sniffed that this was the ultimate conflict of interest for Doc—a sort of "If I can't cure 'em, I'll bury 'em" business plan. But most people paid it no nevermind.

Other relatives had followed Digby to the community, including one of Doc's brothers, who had started up the grocery store, and another cousin of his wife's, who took over the failing cafe. Before he knew it, old Doc had given birth to a sort of dynasty of the cornfields.

The Potluck Dinner that Went Astray

By the time he and his wife died of heart attacks two days apart in 1937, Doc had delivered more than 3,000 babies. He was terribly proud of that!

Ethel had been his only disappointment. She had been a thin and angular child given much to fits of anger and stubbornness. With her boyish hips, she had a sort of sinewy masculinity about her that was more than a tomboy's and an assertiveness that was difficult to mask. Her sharp features and personality had embraced religion with a vengeance at an early age, and she became a pious and devout church-goer.

And Ethel talked a blue streak.

After high school graduation (where she had been the unpopular valedictorian), her folks had packed her off across the state to the Iowa State Teachers College at Cedar Falls to study for what was then one of the few professions open to women. And after college graduation, her mother had taken her off on a grand tour of Europe to round out her education. There she had discovered what was to become the consuming passion in her life.

It started innocently enough. As Ethel and her mother were touring an English churchyard with its dozens of gravestones, she tripped and fell over a rock. After she regained her senses, she found herself sprawled in front of a tombstone that read:

> *As you are now; so once was I;*
> *As I am now; so you shall be;*
> *Therefore prepare to follow me.*

Ethel took the spill and the message to be the result of divine intervention. The Lord had placed that rock there for a reason. She could do little else but follow His lead. And she interpreted that as a calling to study and preserve the wisdom of the dead from centuries past.

So Ethel began her lifelong pursuit of epitaphs and inscriptions on churchyard tombstones. She viewed them as a gift from our ancestors and their kin, where the low and the mighty were commemorated sadly, quietly, expansively—and often with a bit of humor. The memorials were (she said) a priceless and unique heritage—mirrors of the contemporary society of a particular day and a true art form. They were worthy of serious study and contemplation, for they even had some transcendental significance!

The Potluck Dinner that Went Astray

If the truth were known, Ethel also saw in her new avocation a way to avoid teaching, for she had discovered that she had little patience and did not suffer fools gladly. And besides, her father had the money to support her interests, then and in the future, so why not pursue her calling?

So Ethel began traipsing around old graveyards in sensible shoes and a big sun hat. She found in the graveyards a serenity that comforted her soul. In some secret level she found a solace for her discontent and a sweet mourning for her own life.

As she became further transformed, she began to realize that cemeteries offered three wonderful things: history, seasons, and memories. And so she became at home in the land of the dead.

At first she confined her sorties to churchyards in the England she visited every year. She diligently took pictures and copied down the most interesting epitaphs, largely from cemeteries in the southern part of the country. Some were simple couplets such as the one from 1774:

> *Here lies the body of Thomas Proctor,*
> *Who lived and died without a doctor.*

Other epitaphs were sad and told of accidents. A young boy's gravestone in Betchworh from the year 1634 lamented,

> *Dear friends and companions all*
> *Pray warning take from me;*
> *Don't venture on the ice too far*
> *As t'was the death of me.*

And in a little churchyard in Potterne in Wiltshire, she came across this 1790 epitaph that spoke volumes about the relationship between a wife and her husband:

> *Here lies Mary, the wife of John Ford,*
> *We hope her soul is gone to the Lord,*
> *But if for hell she has chang'd this life,*
> *She had better be there than be John Ford's wife!*

Later Ethel expanded her searches to New England in the fall, and on one occasion she traveled to Italy—after boning up on the language. She was disappointed there, however, for she ran into the Italian penchant for poetry and the country's unofficial motto, *se non e vero, e ben trovato*—"it need not be true as long as it is well said."

The Potluck Dinner that Went Astray

Her pictures and stories about the tombstones were carefully preserved in big leatherbound books. She could spend hours showing them off to visitors while chattering away about the adventures she had while she captured the images and words of her ongoing pursuit of the records of immortality.

Ethel lived alone now in her parents' big old house on Spruce Street. No suitors ever came calling. She devoted her energies to her church, her occasional civic duties, and her quest for an understanding of eternity through the study of marble. For companionship, she had her three cats: Shadrach, Meshach, and Abednego.

So it was somewhat of a lonely life, for her single-minded interest and her reputation as a "talker" preceded her wherever she went. The boys down at the pool hall in the little village even made up an epitaph they thought would be appropriate for her own tombstone:

> *Look out Lord, and sing Hallelujah!*
> *Here comes Ethel to tell it to ya!*

Ethel was respected, however, by everyone in town. She could get things done. And this potluck for her nephew Billy was right up her alley. She even had the regard of the members of United Presbyterian Women (UPW), the ladies' organization of the only other church in the little community. And their cooperation certainly was needed if the event was to be a success.

Well sir, some people said that what happened was due to the heat. It had been over 100 degrees for three days, and there was no breeze from the north over the gentle prairie hills.

Some said it was because the affair was so hastily organized; most such things were set up weeks in advance.

Others blamed Ethel's nerves; she hadn't been quite herself since the Carley's dog wet on her rhubarb patch.

The new high school English teacher took a more existential view—something about the confluence of the tides and the moon—while many of the Presbyterian ladies whispered knowingly into their hankies that it was all due to the onset of Ethel's "change of life."

"Shorty" Wilkinson loved to say for years afterward that he had seen it coming. Ethel was once a high school classmate of his who had forgotten that she had a date with him for the Meridan basketball game.

The Potluck Dinner that Went Astray

Whatever the cause, Aunt Ethel simply forgot to phone people and ask them—or assign them—to bring either a salad or a hot dish or rolls or a dessert to the potluck for Billy. And no one noticed!

After all, potlucks were a frequent and routine part of the social fabric of the community and of the two churches. No housewife normally told any other housewife what she was bringing to a potluck. Someone called you, or you signed up on a sheet at the church or wherever, to bring a particular type of food, and that was it—no big deal.

Evidently that's why each housewife was not particularly concerned when Ethel or someone didn't call. Each lady simply figured that she had been inadvertently overlooked and made her plans to attend anyhow. Each one assumed that Ethel had worked out a proper balance between all the salads, hot dishes, rolls, and desserts that everyone was bringing, and that a single contribution wouldn't tip the scale badly one way or the other. So each cook decided she'd bring what she did best, or what her husband liked, or whatever she felt like making.

The result was that at 12:30 P.M. on Sunday, July 23, 1943, as the townfolk gathered under the shade of the four trees near the rusted swingset at the little city park, there were unveiled four Jello salads with marshmallows on top, two pans of rolls, four pies, and twenty-one hot dishes—all of which had baked beans as the primary ingredient! No one knew quite what to do. The Cozy Corner Cafe was closed because Flo and Henry were on vacation, trying to catch walleyes at Lake Wanapeg over the state line in Minnesota. The only other place to get salads or any other food on a Sunday was thirty-five miles away, for heaven's sake.

So there was nothing for it. The Lutheran preacher said grace, and everyone lined up and began filling their plates. In the Christian spirit of things, lots of people didn't take any of the rolls or a piece of pie or any of the salads. Others just took a dab or two of those scarce commodities—to be polite, they said.

The heavy eaters (and there were many, for this was a hard-working farming community) all took a lot of what was most available: hearty portions of the infinite varieties of baked bean casseroles. Some did notice that a few of the ladies' offerings were more popular than others. Presumably, the menfolk who were related to a particular

The Potluck Dinner that Went Astray

housewife recognized the look of a dish and, under the circumstances, opted for the familiar rather than an unknown variation.

There were, of course, some muffled jokes and an occasional burst of laughter from the tables where the men congregated to eat. And a few of the younger school kids ran around chanting "Beans, beans, the musical fruit; the more you eat, the more you toot!" before they were shushed by their mothers.

Aunt Ethel was nearly inconsolable. She sat slumped at one of the picnic tables, dabbing her eyes repeatedly, while the members of the LCW flailed at the air around her with their bamboo fans from Digby's Funeral Parlor. She refused all offers to bring her any food.

Along about three o'clock, most people began to drift away—from one another and from the park. Everybody agreed that Billy looked fine, and they'd all had a good visit. Most of them, however, were beginning to have rumbling stomachs and embarrassed looks on their faces.

Billy said that he had really had a good time, listening to World War I stories about France from cousin Earl and his buddies from the Claude E. Frank American Legion Post #107. But when the news of the potluck menu drifted down to the pool hall, where the guys had the radio tuned to the St. Louis Cardinals baseball game that Sunday afternoon, there were some whoops and a knee slap or two.

Then some other people from neighboring communities picked up the tale, and it became the sole topic of conversation when the farmers came to town on the next Saturday night for grocery-buying and the band concert at villages throughout the county. Some said the Presbyterians spread the tale deliberately. At any rate, it reached Des Moines, and then a radio announcer got ahold of it, and pretty soon it made the Sunday supplement to a Chicago newspaper as one of those "Life in Small Towns" features. It even got a mention in the *Readers Digest!*

Most of the reports played up the Lutheran angle, since the leadership for the affair and Billy himself were of that denomination.

Soon, however, the Baptist and Congregationalist ladies and others who held potluck church dinners began to warn their members about the need for meticulous planning for such events, using the incident as an example of what could happen if one didn't mind her P's and Q's.

But it took the Methodists to finally put a tag on it in a magazine published by the Women's Society of Christian Service (WSCS). The

The Potluck Dinner that Went Astray

national vice president of the WSCS detailed the correct way to organize a potluck dinner, ending with the strong admonition that one should follow the "Four W's" rule to "Write down Who is bringing What and When"!

The editors also included a form that could be copied. It had three columns for *Who, What,* and *When.* In a bit of a dig at their fellow Christians, they titled the sheet "The Lutheran Potluck Form." And they were delighted to explain how it got its name to anyone who asked.

All through the spreading of the tale about the incident, the offices of Lutheran churches throughout the land did their best to ignore the many jokes from their brethren from other denominations and tongue-in-cheek reports in the media. After all, the event had not been an official church function.

But as the negative publicity got more widespread, it even renewed a dissension within the Lutheran Church. The American Lutheran branch began to point a finger at the Missouri Synod branch 'cause Aunt Ethel's church was under that jurisdiction.

Eventually the precept took on the patina and stature of one of Christendom's oldest canons, the "Presbyterian Potluck Rule." That one forbids bringing pickled herring to a Calvinist potluck dinner, because the wife of an elder once read somewhere that Casanova said they were aphrodisiacs.

But the "Lutheran Potluck Rule" transcends the Presbyterian ordinance, for it is truly nondenominational. It should also be applied to even nonreligious gatherings.

And so today you will hear about it today whenever Christian as well as non-Christian ladies gather. It's wise to tape the form by your telephone or on your refrigerator door whenever you're in charge of one of those potluck affairs. Though Aunt Ethel is dead now, she certainly would have appreciated the form, for she was a fine woman who hoped others would profit from her mistakes in life.

And as if to prove that underneath her prim and proper demeanor there lurked an honest and whimsical soul, she had engraved on her tombstone a little gem from a seventeenth-century English churchyard:

> *Beneath this silent stone is laid*
> *A noisy, antiquated maid.*
> *Who from her cradle talked 'til death*
> *And ne'er before was out of breath.*

The Tall Tale of the Little Church that Could

It's called the Old North Church, and it stands at the crossroads of Bread and Cheese Hollow Road and County Highway 17 just over the stream bridge. The white clapboard building with the cupola and bell occupies about ten acres at what is known locally as Roland's Corner. It's situated in one of the more remote parts of the remote state of Maine—in the county of Kennebec in the bucolic Telemakan Lakes area.

The structure is embraced by air that smells of freshness and the tall towering trees of the "north countree" that make the surrounding forest a green cathedral. The little rural church has served the farmers in the area for more than 165 years. It has survived the Pine Tree State's five seasons—fall, winter, spring, summer, and mud—for all those years. And it has remained open through much adversity and affliction—and in that there is a tale.

Originally known as the Old North Meeting House, the building sits on land purchased "in consideration of ten dollars" from a Shadrack Jones and Moses Pennybacker in 1826. The structure was dedicated two years later on a sunny July 18. Its construction was partially furnished by the sale of pews, which went for as little as $4.00 or as much as $32.00—depending on the generosity or the Yankee savvy of the buyer.

Later there was even a sort of market in pews. Some old records indicate that Solomon Simmons was the highest bidder for pew 44, paying $16.50 at a public auction on November 18, 1843.

The building was originally dedicated as a "Calvinist Baptist Church," an apparent outgrowth of the Baptist societies that had been meeting in various homes in the area. It boasted an initial membership of more than 100 people. Elias Wood was its first preacher and served until his death in 1860.

The building of the church was partly the result of the religious revival that swept through America in the early part of the nineteenth century, and for a number of years the little church prospered. The second minister, a Caleb P. Jennings, taught school in the nearby one-

The Potluck Dinner that Went Astray

room country schoolhouse in the winter months. He presided over the first wedding in the little structure in April of 1867. It made legitimate the whispered-about liaison of the granddaughter of one of the original settlers in the area, Eliphalet Burton.

Burton was a one-legged veteran of the Revolutionary War. He had been a young fifer at Valley Forge, one of three musicians from the area who had been in the Continental Army. Burton was a Quaker, however, and was tossed out of the Society of Friends for receiving a military pension. So when the old man died, his relatives had him buried in the cemetery adjacent to Old North, with the Reverend Jennings presiding at the funeral. After some discussion, the family—with frugal Down East prudence—decided not to bury his old fife and wooden leg with him, in the event someone in the family might later have a use for them.

The Quakers were but one denomination in an increasingly competitive religious area. Although the Friends had their meeting house about three miles down Route 17, the Congregationalists built a church directly catty-corner from Old North at Roland's Corner in 1872, on land donated by Silas Esterman. About the same time, his son Bud started up a general store at the crossroads.

Bud liked exotic names, and when his only daughter was born, he named her Pneumonia. He had seen it in print and liked the way it looked—sort of classy, he thought. He moved his lips lovingly as he said it to himself: "Pee-nee-oo-moan-ya." By the time somebody pointed out how it was really pronounced, it was too late. The poor girl went through life named after a malady. She grew up to manage the store, however, and later her descendants took it over. But the place was always called "Bud's."

The addition of the all-purpose country store to the dusty crossroads in the mid-1870s threatened to turn the little junction into a village. But better county roads and the arrival of the railroad in Telemakan two miles away squashed any ambitions some folk had for such an eventuality.

The two churches quietly competed for members, though, until the 1890s. When Old North started a Sunday School one year, the Congregationalists followed suit. When Fanny Yeaton donated money for two station agent stoves to warm the Congregational church, Effie Peabody did the same for Old North. And when Old North got a used

The Tall Tale of the Little Church that Could

pump organ, the Congregationalists prevailed upon Hattie Twogood to donate—and play—a brand new "cottage" organ.

On some Sunday mornings, the resulting musical competition was loud enough to unsettle the cows in the adjacent fields. In fact, their moos sometimes joined in on a hymn or two. The churches were only about 100 yards across the road from one another, and in the still country air, voices—and organ music—carried.

Some of the Congregationalists were former Methodists and took John Wesley's admonition to sing lustily and with courage quite seriously. The Reverend Jennings' flock, though, was not to be outdone. On one memorable Sabbath—by sheer coincidence—the congregations started up on "Bringing in the Sheaves" at the very same time, which moved the cows to join in as a sort of bovine chorus. People said that even sinners all the way down to Telemakan heard the combined version. Some of them viewed it as a Christian plot designed to lure them out into the countryside and into the fold of one church or the other.

In spite of the competition, there was some cooperation between the churches. Both churches were saved by the heroic efforts of their congregations during the Big Fire of 1885. Following a long dry spell, much of the wooded area around them burned for a week. And after its members had ensured that Old North was safe from the flames, they hurried across the road to help their Congregational neighbors.

The churches survived the fire, but neither church could withstand the diphtheria epidemic of 1878. It took the lives of at least ten school children, and even though the teacher of the District 16 school survived, she was "despaired of."

This event seemed to trigger a decline in both congregations. People began to move away into the more civilized confines of Telemakan and other towns, and some even moved to Augusta. The congregations began to age, and new members became hard to come by for both churches. By 1898, the Congregationalists were down to about twenty members, and the closing of their sanctuary was inevitable.

Old North wasn't doing much better. The once-sparkling model of a New England church had been reduced to what many called "a weather-beaten old barn" due to a lack of maintenance. Something had

The Potluck Dinner that Went Astray

to be done, and when the Congregationalists approached them with a proposition to combine forces, the Old North congregation listened.

Things move rather slowly in the Maine countryside, but after two years of negotiation, the two churches merged. The new entity was incorporated as the "Federated New North Church," and it was officially nondenominational. In becoming a sort of general Protestant church, the congregations became part of a growing movement in rural areas at the time, where folks of different denominations—whose numbers were not large enough to maintain their own church—joined together to worship God on a nondenominational basis.

The new entity decided to use the Old North structure as their sanctuary. The only restriction placed on the use of the property by the former congregation was that the newly established congregation had to promise to continue to follow the Baptist tradition of immersion when someone was baptized.

So volunteer labor set about restoring the old building. The women raised money for the remodeling by serving chicken pot pie suppers in the sanctuary. People sat in the pews and balanced their plates on their knees. The men donated their labor, and the Ladies Aid Society was formed. The ladies worked hard at naggin' the fellas to refurbish the church.

The Congregational Church was torn down and the lumber used to repair Old North and to build a little Sunday School building out back. The steeple and bell were added to the structure at this time, and Guy Yeaton climbed up on the roof and used a long-handled pitchfork to place the weather vane at the very top of the steeple. Everybody cheered!

During the five years it took to restore the building, however, a number of minor accidents took place. One day while hammerin' down some shingles, Alhanan Worthy fell off a ladder and broke his hip. And young Billy Westfall spilt a whole bucket of white paint on ol' Mrs. Jergin's head one Saturday afternoon.

But finally, on June 18 in the year of our Lord 1905, the new building was dedicated. It was a glorious occasion! People remembered later that the minister—the Reverend Lucius Packard, who had been ordained in the Methodist church—preached a mighty fine sermon all about hope and faith. And later the people enjoyed strawberries and ice cream.

The Tall Tale of the Little Church that Could

But as the century moved on, even the newly combined congregation continued to dwindle. Two young male members joined the American Expeditionary Forces (AEF) in 1918, went to fight in France, and never returned. They weren't killed or anything like that, but as the popular song of the day had it, "How Ya' Gonna' Keep 'Em Down on the Farm, after They've Seen Paree?"

During the Depression years, the congregation paid the minister in produce and hand-me-down clothing, and there was a real struggle to buy the necessary things to keep the church open. The country school was closed in 1935, and more folks retired or lost their farms and moved to town.

Church attendance started to swell in the summer though, when the summer complaints (as city people were called) who had begun to build seasonal cabins at the nearby ponds (as lakes were called) came to the worship services. These visitors (from what the natives called "Away") were cautiously welcomed. One of them later made the area famous with a play and movie he called *On Golden Pond*. But attendance by the year-round residents continued to dwindle, as the young people graduated from Telemakan High in town and moved away to jobs or college.

One of the youngsters did make the church members momentarily happy by contemplating a career in the ministry, but it gradually came to him that such a pursuit called for more restraint in the fringe benefits of life than he was willing to assume—and so he ended up majoring in biology.

Anyway, the little church managed to stay open during World War II, and the entire congregation, which was down to only about thirty families by then, gathered to mourn the death of one of their own. Billy Westfall's son was killed at Amchitka in the Aleutian Islands off Alaska.

During those war years, the congregation made some further improvements in the building. There were, however, some misunderstandings and foot-dragging. When the minister asked for extra donations in 1944 to replace the chandelier, there some grumblings by the members. After all, complained one old-timer, nobody really knew how to play the one they already had, and besides the money might better be spent doing something about the poor lighting in the place!

The Potluck Dinner that Went Astray

But after World War II, the church could no longer afford such improvements or even a resident pastor, and so the members had to rely on vacationing ministers and professors of religion from branches of the University of Maine to supply the pulpit. Still, the faithful kept the little church open.

Miss Penelope Dose was the much-maligned organist for more than thirty years, and Clyde T. Mellinger followed his father and grandfather as the sexton, who cleaned and maintained the building. And the great-granddaughter of the girl who had been the first to marry in the little church was a faithful worshiper every Sunday.

Even they had to concede defeat in 1960, however, when the continued decline in membership and poor attendance in the wintertime forced the trustees of the Federated New North Church Corporation to close the place every fall. They opened it up for Christmas Eve services and then shut the doors again until June when the summer complaints arrived.

The little church did receive a boost from an unlikely source. A famous beauty expert (who the locals said had enough money to burn a wet elephant) established a health retreat for celebrities on a pond about five miles from the church. The natives called it a "fat farm," but it was also a drying-out place for alcoholic actresses and other notables who spent their summer days in a strict regimen designed to purge their bodies of toxins.

The proprietress (who was originally a Baptist from Sioux City, Iowa) also believed in the redemptive power of prayer and the healing nature of religion. So on many Sundays in the summer, she loaded her charges into the establishment's big vans and took them to the little nondenominational country church.

Well sir, word got around that one could star gaze at Old North in the summertime, and the sanctuary was filled on many a Sabbath morning. People who hadn't been to any church in years flocked to the place to gaze open-mouthed at the famous. Some drove out from Augusta for the day.

The place got so crowded on some mornings that it moved one local parishioner to unknowingly paraphrase Gertrude Stein to the effect that there was no more away, Away. But in keeping with true Maine demeanor, no one bothered the celebrities or asked for autographs. The locals respected their privacy and were content to just gape.

The Tall Tale of the Little Church that Could

The packed houses on some Sundays proved to be something of a bonanza for the finances of Old North. People who were not used to attending church and were intimidated by the ritual of the collection plate often gave generously.

One of the ushers told of a citified visitor in a blue blazer who pulled out his wallet and was contemplating the two twenties and two one-dollar bills in it as the collection started. A coupla' dollars apparently seemed too little, and a twenty too much. Just then the collection plate reached him, and, flustered and in haste, he pulled out the two twenties and dropped 'em both in the plate.

The coffers of the church were enriched by such events, and the health farm owner also became a major contributor, even though the cynics among the members sniffed that she probably deducted her generous offering every Sunday as a business expense. But the trustees eventually had enough money to replace the original pew cushions and re-carpet the floor of the sanctuary.

Although the sexton was there when the workmen from Bill's Carpets out of Augusta unscrewed and took out the pews in preparation for replacing the carpet, he was sick the day they installed it. And so no one noticed until it was too late that the workers had carpeted over the wooden lid above the old baptismal (or tub, as some heretics called it).

When the error was discovered, the trustees shrugged it off. No one had been baptized in the church in more than twenty years, and no one was likely to be in the future. Nope, let it go, they said. Not to worry.

But they hadn't counted on the owner of the health farm. She had two daughters, and one of them recently became a mother. The young mother wanted—in fact demanded—her child to be baptized at the country church she had come to visit and love each summmer. And as she reminded the trustees, she and her mother and sister had been most generous in their support of the little church.

What to do? The agreement about baptisms at the church was still in force. It was contained in a legal document, and although the paper was more than seventy-five years old, some former Baptist people in the congregation had long memories. Besides, this was an honest, Christian organization.

The Potluck Dinner that Went Astray

Any baptism performed at the church just had to be by immersion. And the only way to do that was to tear up the new carpet over the lid of the old baptismal.

The trustees took the matter "under advisement." To the repeated and impatient questioning of the young mother, they said they were "working on it." When their deliberations stretched out over two summers though, the mother began to despair. Her kid would be in junior high before the event took place, she said.

Finally, after some discussions that were longer than a hard winter, the trustees reached a decision. They would turn the entire matter over to the sexton—who most people blamed for the situation in the first place. "If he hadn't been sick the day they installed the carpet . . . " went the reasoning. More than likely he was hung over again, some said.

Clyde T. Mellinger was a tippler. Although he was a God-fearin' man, he was also a connoisseur of the local raw moonshine called "WHEW!" And he liked—as he put it—to get an edge on. He was also a character. His sister often said that if he was any older, they'd call him eccentric.

Clyde was a short, lean fellow with a ruddy tinge, a love of life, a fertile imagination, and a fountain of stories. He was also, by his own estimation, a champion horseshoe pitcher. His full-time occupation, however, was farming, and evidently the time he spent doing routine tasks on a tractor or milking the cows gave him time to ponder and conjure.

He took over the family farm during his teens, even though folks said he was so bowlegged that he couldn't stop a pig in an alley. He started his jawin' about then, but he only began to lie in earnest when he got to his fifties. And that's when he became one of the all-time greats, ya' might say.

Most of Clyde's stories were preposterous tests of the imagination that challenged the listener to find the truth in them. Although they were loosely based on facts, the exaggerated humor gave folks an opportunity to laugh at themselves and their problems. They typically described a person overcoming the region's rugged terrain and harsh climate with Yankee ingenuity and revealed a tangy, flinty sense of the philosophical. The tales exaggerated the problems, but also exaggerated the ability of the rural folk to handle the problems.

The Tall Tale of the Little Church that Could

The stories were delivered in a high-pitched voice and a laconic, broad "A" Yankee accent, which unto themselves were enough to make people smile. The final "r" in a word was usually replaced with an "ah" or "uh" ("there" became "thay-ah," and "near" got to be "nee-uh"). And he added an "r" to people's names when their parents unaccountably forgot ("Lucinda" became "Lucinder" in Clyde's mouth). His yarns were usually long, but his sentences were—in typical Down East style—a mite short, for he did admire an economy in words. The local paper once described Clyde as "Telemakan's taciturn teller of tall tales."

He had also achieved some fame by posting a sign in one of his pastures near County Road 17. It read:

Don't cross this field unless you can do it in 9.9 seconds.
The bull can do it in 10.

Clyde started an "Adopt-a-Cow" program for the summer complaint people from Away. Its purpose was to provide a cruelty-free life for a cow and to help it avoid the slaughterhouse. For $10 a month you got an adoption certificate, a photo of your bossy, an emblazoned T-shirt and cap, and a newsletter to keep you up-to-date on your animal. You also got a mimeographed vegetarian cookbook. Clyde called it "the most revolutionary cow protection program in the world!" Even though he got it listed in the book *Gifts that Make a Difference* (which had national distribution), he didn't sell many memberships.

When his hay crop was ruined by a sudden downpour one year, he phoned the weather girl at the Augusta television station and fired her. "Shouldn't have the job if she couldn't do better than that," he opined—and hung up. He was also the originator of the sign at Bud's General Store that said, "If We Don't Have It, You Don't Need It!"

His family had been members of the Old North Baptist congregation for generations, and when it came to baptisms, Clyde averred as how even the Congregationalists had originally practiced immersion. They proved so inept at it, however, that they drowned somebody. That's what started their little sprinkle-on-the-head routine, he said.

Clyde had also been involved in the last baptism that had taken place at Old North in 1967. Early on that cold January morning, he had lit the little boiler that warmed the water in the baptismal and had gone home to finish his chores. When he returned just before church

The Potluck Dinner that Went Astray

time and saw the steam rising from the opening, he hastily organized a bucket brigade among the members who were just arriving for services. They commandeered buckets and water from Bud's store across the way to replace the scalding hot liquid with some cold water, while the cautious minister kept testing the temperature with his elbow. Church services were delayed for about thirty minutes while Clyde and the others scurried about, but otherwise, as he put it, "there would sure as hell been one parboiled parishioner and one cooked parson!"

So Clyde took on the charge to find some sort of solution to the current crisis over the baptism of the grandchild of the health farm owner. To inquiries, he allowed as how he was "studying on it."

To simply cut a hole in the carpet around the 3' x 8' lid wouldn't work, 'cause the carpet was an inexpensive indoor/outdoor type of some sort of fiberglass-like material, and big polyester strings would be hangin' out all around the sides. Even if they trimmed 'em off, it would look awful.

To cut off the carpet in the front half of the church near the altar, where the baptismal was located, would also leave strings all the way across the sanctuary, and the partial carpet would look even worse. And to replace the entire carpet with new and more expensive material was out of the question.

But in what he later called one of his "Eureka Moments," Clyde came upon the solution. He reached this epiphany while settin' on the john one morning, and it was so obvious it made his head swim.

The agreement of many years ago said that all baptisms on the church property had to be by immersion. "On the church property," it said—not "in the church." So why not dig a little hole in the yard, fill it with water, and do the deed there? After all, the grounds were church property!

They'd fill in the hole afterwards, and in this way the carpet would be untouched. And the chances that anyone else would ever want to be baptized in the little building in the future were just about as likely as the Pope havin' a baby—eh? Besides, by that time it would then be someone else's worry! Praise God!

Clyde presented his solution at a specially called meeting of the trustees, and they bought it. "Well, I'll be!" said one, when Clyde showed him the part about "the property" in the agreement. And with a unanimous "Ayuh," they even authorized him to hire a local contractor to dig the hole. So Clyde got ahold of Jay's Construction Company

The Tall Tale of the Little Church that Could

over to Telemakan and set up an appointment to have them come out and dig up the grounds. And he laid out a 3' x 8' plot with four stakes, out by the old Sunday School building.

On the appointed day, however, Clyde had another one of his headaches. And he didn't know that some kids had pulled up three of the stakes to use in making rubber guns.

So, when Otis Englebert from Jay's Construction arrived on his small Caterpillar at seven o'clock that morning to dig the hole, there was only one stake and no Clyde. Ordinarily, this would have been no problem, but "Open-Mouth Otis," as he was called, was a bit slow. Even in mosey-along Maine, it usually took five or six seconds before a statement by anybody got through to his brain. Folks said he was "such a zero that he didn't know enuf to set down when he was tired." His boss agreed with his mother in allowin' as how he had always been about a quart low.

Otis looked at the stake, which he presumed marked a starting point for the hole, and at his work order. It said "3 x 8, dig hole." But by what measurements? Feet, yards, rods? Otis had just come off a job in which the dimensions were measured in rods, and this being a church—and what with all that stuff about a rod and a staff in some half-forgotten prayer from his childhood—he settled on rods.

One of the trustees was driving home in his pickup about six o'clock that evening and nearly ran off the road at the sight of Otis just finishing up his work for the day. There it was: a gaping hole gouged in the earth by the side of the little church, a hole 3 x 8 rods. That is 19 yards wide and 44 yards long!

Fortunately, Otis had remembered that somebody had mentioned that this was to be a pool or somethin', and he had made the arbitrary decision to limit the depth to about three feet. He had it all figured out that if they wanted it deeper, he'd come back.

But what was the little church to do with a hole that was half the size of a football field in its side yard? The trustees met in an emergency session that night and sought out Clyde, but repeated calls to his farmhouse went unanswered. Even his sister didn't know where he was. Someone must have told him about the fiasco, and after one look he had skedaddled.

The trustees were undone. Gloom descended on them. So they decided to cast their burden upon the Lord, and after a round of

The Potluck Dinner that Went Astray

prayers, they all got up feeling better. The matter was now out of their hands. Their petitions must have worked, for when Clyde surfaced a few weeks later, he claimed to have a solution to all their problems. He said it came to him on the merry-go-round in an amusement park, up back of Bangor. Praise God!

Instead of bemoaning their fate, they should embrace it, he said! They should hearken to an ancient Greek word he had found in an old dictionary: *epichairekakia*. It meant "rejoicing over calamities."

All they had to do, he told 'em, was to fill up the hole with water! They could use it as a wadin' pool in the summer and a skatin' rink in the winter! And they could charge admission and use the money to support the church! Couldn't be simpler! Wicked easy! Praise God!

The trustees looked at one another. Clyde was obviously now seriously deranged. He had gone 'round the bend this time. The incident had simply been some too much for him. The old faht was bahmy! Teched! Bonkers! Either that or he had got ahold of a bad batch of WHEW!

But don't cha' know, the more they chewed it over, the more it started to make a wild sort of sense. For in spite of all the ponds in the region, there were no sandy beaches and shallow waters where little kids could frolic. Some of the adult summer complaints couldn't swim but loved the water and would probably like to wade around in a really true little pond.

And there sure as hell wasn't much joint recreational activity around there during the winter months when the Montreal Express came blowin down. People tended to hunker down and stay put 'cause it was so cold—according to Clyde—that a 33-degree Mason often dropped to 4 below!

So as they mulled it over and stirred it up and looked at it this way and that, they began to see the possibilities. They could get some sand and build a little beach at one end of the hole and then fill it with water. In the winter time when it froze over, they could string some lights, and build a bonfire, and turn it into a skating rink for the locals!

In the summer, the two high school kids in the congregation could watch over the customers as sort of junior life guards. The Ladies Aid could make and sell refreshments to the patrons out of the old Sunday School house.

In the winter they could use the old house as a warming hut and dispense hot chocolate and cider for kids and adults. "And," cried

The Tall Tale of the Little Church that Could

Mabel Witterberg in a burst of enthusiasm, "We can call the whole thing EPICHAIREKAKIA!"

It will give everybody something to learn to pronounce, she gushed After all, didn't Mark Twain give his children names like Zoroaster and Blatherstrike so that they would learn to handle hard words? Eh?

So they got the county cooperative extension agent from over to Ogoonquite to help them draw up plans and advise them about preparing the hole for water and how to keep it clean and circulating. And lo and behold, they discovered that the evacuation had unveiled a little spring from the nearby stream that would keep the water fresh, and then they really became some excited!

So they got Jay of Jay's Construction Company to sell them the sand at wholesale prices because he was still feeling a bit guilty about his company's role in the original catastrophe. And they made arrangements with Bud's General Store to buy pop and ice cream at cost for resale to their hoped-for customers.

Finally on one Saturday and Sunday in July of 1988, they filled the hole up with water, using a hose connected to the sink in the old schoolhouse. And by God, it worked!

So they erected a big red sign that said WELCOME TO EPICHAIREKAKIA! out by the driveway off Route 17 and sent out some flyers to all the summer complaints in the area. And people—toting kids—turned out.

Oh, it wasn't any Disney World, and after the initial flush of customers, attendance sort of leveled off. But many parents dropped their little ones off for an afternoon or when they went to town to shop. And over time, the little pond became a part of summmerin' in Maine for many families. It was—as they said in those parts—"elegant" and of the "finest kind."

But after a few weeks of low patronage by the locals in the wintertime, the trustees decided to open it only on Friday and Saturday nights during that season. They did try to encourage its use on other occasions by starting a kids hockey team. And to make amends for his blunder, "Open-Mouth" Otis volunteered to put on his Mackinaw and be the coach. But when they gave him a hockey puck, he spent the rest of the day trying to open it.

The Potluck Dinner that Went Astray

Someone then remembered that Otis had once claimed that all sorts of cats and dogs had dropped on him during a heavy rainstorm, and because he was the only one to volunteer for the coach's job, they gave up the idea. Eventually, the trustees only staffed the pond in the winter on Saturday evenings.

But EPICHAIREKAKIA! continues to make a little money every year, largely through the concession sales in the summer. The income has allowed the church to keep its doors open to serve the people of God—all year 'round now!

Even the locals who aren't members drive by the place nowadays with grins of admiration. They've taken to calling it "the little church that could!"

There will undoubtedly be another crisis that will threaten the existence of the little church. But it has survived many trials and tribulations over the past 165 years, and it bids fair to survive many more.

It will survive because of Baptist optimism, Congregational self-determination, and the wonderful and enduring faith of its members. God truly works in wondrous ways!

So says Clyde T. Mellinger, who's retired now and loves to tell this tall tale of "advencha" to anybody who stops by his wheelchair at the Oakdale Nursing Home in Augusta. He swears this one is true—sorta.

And, he adds, they never did baptize the granddaughter of the health farm owner. By the time they got around to it, she had closed the establishment permanently, and she never returned to Maine.

The Praying Pigs

If you're a member of a mainstream Protestant church, you have probably noticed that there is no personal praying out loud by any of the people attending the services on a Sunday morning. The "Lord's Prayer" in unison is usually about the extent of it. Sometimes everyone reads together a new prayer of confession that is printed in the bulletin, but there is usually no extemporaneous, impromptu appeal to God by any individual members. That's left for the minister. Aand there's a reason for it.

It seems there were such goings-on, particularly in the southern branches of many Protestant churches prior to the 1970s. The stalwart souls down there were sort of influenced by the Free Methodists and the Baptists, and the practice even got picked up by "The Frozen Chosen," as the Presbyterians are sometimes called.

But a series of events catapulted individual, out-loud prayer by southern Presbyterians into some unwanted and disastrous publicity that spread to other religions. And so that church and most of the other denominations had to (at least informally) call a halt to the practice throughout the United States.

Evidently it all started when three pre-ministerial students from that venerable Presbyterian institution, Toskaloosa College, were motoring back to the school at Grabmiss, Tennessee, after Thanksgiving recess. The boys had been doing a missionary bit at the Good Shepherd Sunquest Senior Village at Biloxi, Mississippi, over the holidays and were returning to their classes. To pass the time, they got to discussing some of the more weighty theological issues they were studying that semester. One of the vexing questions they were having to deal with in Professor Jenkins' class was the nature of the soul. It all seemed to boil down to "what was it and who had it." The blacks claimed to have more of it than other folk, but what it was was hard to define.

That got them to speculating even more about the nature of things and pondering such imponderables such as whether the tree falling in the forest made a sound if no one was there and whether a cat was washing its face or washing its hands and drying them on its face. That last conundrum got them all so hungry that they decided to pull in at the truck stop in Benson, Mississippi, for some burgers and fries.

The Potluck Dinner that Went Astray

They were still talking about the cat when they plumped down in a booth at Sam's Place and were so intent in their discussion that they barely noticed the two waitresses who operated the joint for the owner. The girls were charter members of what Tom Robbins calls the "Sisters of the Daily Special." One of them had hair that had a life of its own, and her most passionate wish was to find a man—any man—who didn't answer "10-4" every time she said something to him.

She took the boys' orders and flirted a bit with the older one. Both girls listened to their talk and were impressed. By this time, the fellows were into all sorts of speculation about animal husbandry. The youngest was sure that since every living creature was God's creation, they all had souls. After all, didn't the Catholics have a day when the priest put on his finest raiment to bless the animals that people brought to church? And wasn't there a Lutheran minister in Germany who was famous for baptizing cats?

Now, if the girls hadn't been interested in the boys, none of the subsequent events would have occurred. But Thelma had taken a shine to the older boy, and though she wasn't what you'd call a regular churchgoer, she had been raised a Baptist and knew her Mama would like to have a parson in the family.

So from behind the counter, she volunteered the first information about Henry Harper to anyone from outside Yoknapatawpha County. "Yew guys oughta go see an ol' farmer neah heah," she said. "He teaches his pigs how ta pray."

Well sir, that stopped the boys in their tracks. It turned out that Henry's little farm was only about six miles down County Road 7 after you turned left off the highway at the fireworks stand. The boys gulped down the rest of their Cokes and left a ten-cent tip and two disappointed girls.

When they saw the mailbox that said "Harper" and turned down the lane that led to the little house, they were amazed at the neatness of the place. One of the boys, who was raised on a farm, remarked that pig farming was the dirtiest, foulest, stinkingest kind of farming that ever was. Even though the house and barn were old and weather-beaten, there was an air of tidiness about the spread.

The group found Henry out by the barn, repairing a harness for his mule. He seemed to be about sixty years-old, and his thin black face sported a little white beard and an almost shocking white head of hair. He was dressed in immaculate bib overalls and big rubber boots.

The Praying Pigs

The boys explained their reason for being there, careful to call him "Mr. Harper." He said he only did his prayer teaching at feeding time, for he wanted his animals to be grateful for what they were about to receive. Glancing at the shadows, he allowed as how that would be in an hour or two. So they all moseyed over to the porch of the little house where Mrs. Harper served them some lemonade 'cause it was hot.

Mr. Harper explained that he had started the prayers after reading a tale in the Bible about a demented man by the name of Legion. Jesus transferred the man's "unclean spirits" into 2,000 swine, which promptly rushed down a slope into the sea where they drowned. Since Mr. Harper's livelihood depended on porkers, he didn't want that to happen to his little herd, and he decided that prayer—particularly at mealtime—might forestall such an event.

One of the lads asked if he'd ever thought of teaching them to sing. Henry said no 'cause he followed the old advice that you should never try to teach a pig how to warble 'cause it simply wastes your time and annoys the pig.

The little group spent the rest of the time chewing over the situation in silence. Henry seemed content with the boys' presence, and they didn't know what else to say.

Finally, with a look to the sky, Henry struggled to his feet and went around the side of the house where his wife handed him a pail. He waved for the boys to follow him, explaining that the potato peelings, turnip tops, and other kitchen debris in the container were this evening's treats for the swine.

When Henry entered the sty, he was up over his ankles in black Mississippi goo. The four boars and sows and their piglets knew what time it was and pushed and shoved one another to get to the trough, while Henry quickly spread some feed around and topped it off with the contents of the pail. He then began a sort of sing-song chant in a rich, black patois, which sounded something like this:

> *Hush, hush, hoggies,*
> *Pray for what we have,*
> *This is for our good.*
> *Hush, hush*
> *And is from the land*
> *Hush, hoggies, hush*
> *Blessed be the Lord.*
> *Amen and Amen and Amen!*

The Potluck Dinner that Went Astray

The hogs seemed to be having none of it, however, and kept rushing the trough to get at the food while Henry beat them back with a cane. The pigs were snorting and grunting and oinking and churning up the mud, and Henry kept beating them back and slipping and sliding and stumbling around the enclosure. By now he was shouting to be heard, for the din was frightful! When it reached a crescendo, Henry evidently believed the message had gotten through, the pigs had responded, the Lord's will had been done—and so he withdrew from the field.

He said he'd been doing his thing with the hogs for about thirty-five years, now.

The boys were silent for most of the rest of the way back to Toscaloosa, but the next day they told Professor Jenkins about their experience. They asked him whether he thought pigs could pray. Jenkins showed a great deal of interest in the question because he was coming up for tenure the next year and was looking for a good research project that would impress the committee and the chairman of his department. It was publish-or-perish time, and his best friend kept reminding him of the old academic bromide that noted while Jesus was a great teacher, he didn't publish—and look what happened to him!

So Prof Jenkins returned to Henry's place with the boys and observed first-hand all the goings-on at feeding time. He came away persuaded that the hogs understood Henry's prayers and were, in fact, responding to them and joining in with some of their own. He couldn't identify the language they were using, however, but he was sure some further study would reveal the dialect. Henry was a member of the African Methodist Episcopal Church, so maybe the pigs were too.

So when the professor got back to Tusculum, he drew up a research proposal for a grant to a private foundation to study the matter and, as was required, submitted it to the Vice President of Business Affairs. Even though Tusculum College was one of the oldest coeducational colleges associated with the Presbyterian church, there wasn't very much outside-funded research done at the school, and the vice-president kept hearing about all the overhead charges that were tacked on to grant proposals by the big research universities. He needed $8,000 to fix the roof of the president's house, so with a snicker he added a modest 25 percent to the grant request as "overhead" and sent it across the hall for the president's signature.

The Praying Pigs

The president was preoccupied with a dispute between two professors over a parking space the day the proposal reached his desk, and he signed the document without reading much of it. And so a $32,000 grant request to try to make the unintelligible animal sounds intelligible arrived up at the Merill Endowment in Indianapolis with the official seal of Toskaloosa College in Grabmiss, Tennessee, affixed thereto.

The Merill Endowment was well-known for its funding of religious studies, but this one was a bit unusual. It had the good fortune, however, to land on the desk of a new young program officer by the name of Muriel Peto. She was sort of a "My Friend Irma" with a degree, who had been secretly in love with Rex Harrison ever since she saw him in *Doctor Dolittle* a few years back. If Rex could talk to the animals, why couldn't this little ol' black man down in Mississippi? Moreover, why couldn't they pray back at him? After all, wasn't there something in the Bible about Mary sharing the stable with talking animals? And didn't the birds reportedly enjoy the sermons of Francis of Assisi? So she approved the grant request and sent it in to the president of the endowment.

Now it so happened that the foundation was under some pressure from the IRS that year, because the expenditures for staff salaries, maintenance of the facilities, and general operations had greatly exceeded its grant-giving in the previous year. The foundation had to square it up with the Feds by making a lot more grants this year, so the president signed off on the request without really looking at it. Thus, one day in June of 1977, a check for $32,000 arrived at Toskaloosa College to support research "into the language used by porcines in prayer."

Armed with the funds, Professor Jenkins led the three boys back to Benson for some organized field research. They camped on the lawn out back of Henry's house, and each morning and evening for two solid months that summer they watched and recorded the sounds of Henry slopping his hogs. They studied the intensity of the muck on different days and how the weather affected the responses of the animals. They gave names to each one, as well as to the new little piglets, and did individual psychological profiles. They even studied the sex lives of the sows and boars for clues.

After filling a van full of data, the researchers returned to Toskaloosa that fall to sort it all out. Setting up a lab in the physics

The Potluck Dinner that Went Astray

building, they pored over the audiotapes, notebooks, thermometer readings, and mud samples. They broke down the individual pig sounds, using the phonetic alphabet, and studied the phonemes and compared them to every known language on earth. What were they saying, and in what language? Had Henry really taught them how to pray?

There seemed to be no answer. They couldn't make heads nor tails out of any of the stuff.

After six months of six-days-a-week labor, the professor and the students were at an impasse, and the grant money was running out. Professor Jenkins was getting tired of the gibes of his fellow academicians at the faculty club about the unrewarding nature of his research.

One morning, however, two well-dressed men in dark suits were waiting for him when he unlocked his office door. They said they were from the Pentagon and were "here about the swine." It seemed that the CIA had read about the research in the Merill Endowment Annual Report and tipped off the Department of Defense.

The Pentagon was interested in the project because (1) if the hogs were using an identifiable but obscure language, the Army could teach people to speak it in order to hide troop movements from the enemy, just like they did in World War II when Navajo Indians were used as radio operators in the South Pacific; and (2) if the hogs were speaking in an unknown language, our people had to learn it before—God forbid—the Russians did. Nothing less than the national security was at stake here!

So the agents asked Professor Jenkins if he could use some more money—say, a couple of million or so—to continue his research. And they promised all the logistical support he needed.

Well, of course, Jenkins said he'd be "delighted." He knew that, based on their experience with the Merill Endowment, the college had established new research rates of 50 percent for overhead at Toskaloosa. Such funds would enable the school to pay off all the debt of the athletic department, thereby making his brother-in-law (the football coach) very happy.

Armed with the seemingly unlimited funds, Professor Jenkins dropped the three boys and his other student help and hired a number of full-time professional linguists. They got a gift from Hormel, the nation's top pork-producing company up in Austin, Minnesota, and built a spanking new building that was dedicated one Sunday as the

The Praying Pigs

"Spam Sound Research Hall." It housed a bunch of sophisticated state-of-the-art electronic gear that was capable of breaking down sounds into milli-microseconds.

A veritable army of researchers descended on Benson and camped out in a tent city in Henry's meadow that year, supplied by the Army's 5th Brigade from Fort Bragg. By this time, some of the original animals had matured and gone to market, so they had to begin all over with the new piglets while continuing to monitor the old boars and sows—which by now they were distinguishing by calling them barrows (males) and gilts (females).

The researchers studied and recorded every movement and sound of the animals for nine months, sending volumes of notes and tapes and observations back to the Toskaloosa campus. There, experts in language and linguistics from all over the world broke down the pigs' sounds, grunt by grunt, snort by snort, and oink by oink.

They discovered that the animals had a vocabulary of twenty different tones, and that their squeals ranged from 110 to 115 decibels—about the level of a jet taking off at an airport. But the researchers still couldn't identify the language.

The breakthrough came when Robin MacNeil, the PBS (Public Broadcasting System) news reporter, happened to hear some excerpts from one of the tapes on "All Things Considered" on NPR (National Public Radio). He was deep into the research for his book and television series, The Story of English, and immediately identified the pigs' language as an early and primitive form of English slang spoken by an obscure clan in the Highlands of Scotland in the sixteenth century. He wouldn't hazard a guess as to how it got to hogs in Mississippi, though.

Armed with that information, Professor Jenkins flew in linguists from Scotland and called upon the services of Professor Gather B. Hassaday of the University of Wisconsin, the nation's expert on the history and source of regional slang.

The new team studied the matter for another three months and finally came to a conclusion. At a news conference attended by more than twenty-five press, radio, and television reporters on May 7, 1970, Professor Jenkins announced that the porkers were speaking Presbyterian!

True, it was an early and now-archaic form of Calvinist speech, but there was no doubt that the snorts and whines and wheezes and

The Potluck Dinner that Went Astray

grunts were parts of a crude but authentic Presbyterian speech pattern. They had traced it back to a rare breed of Gloucester Old Spot pigs that are currently supported by the Rare Breeds Survival Trust and its patron, Prince Charles.

How the language got to Mississippi was another matter. The prevailing theory was that some of the swine that were imported into a colony on Long Island in 1735 spoke the lingo, and it was somehow handed down to their descendants in Mississippi 250 years later. But the academicians cautioned that such a transference was but a postulation on their part. They said the pigs seemed to be praying—sort of. Some of the grunts could be interpreted as an "Amen!" and "Praise be!"—at least that's what the researchers thought.

Well, sir, the furor over the discovery was enormous! Intrepid television newscasters descended on old Henry's farm from all over the world and did standups in the middle of the pig sty. Hundreds of people came to see the pigs pig out! The crowds got so big at the morning and evening feedings that bleachers had to be erected. Many people wanted to see an African Methodist Episcopal and some Presbyterians praying together, 'cause it was an unprecedented and historic event.

Henry's minister preached, and the choir from his church sang and shouted "hallelujahs!" and ran the concession stands. The two boars, however, began to get a big head over all the attention and tried to get out of the pen and root for truffles under the oak tree. And during all of the hullabaloo, one of the sows died and presumably went off to hot dog heaven.

But a four-minute video titled *Hush Hoggies Hush: Henry Harper's Praying Pigs,* produced by the Center for the Study of Southern Folklore in Nashville, won a bronze plaque at the Columbus (Ohio) Film Festival. And it was awarded a Vidi as "The Most Unusual Program of the Year 1979" by the National Video Clearinghouse Incorporated.

Some folk around the country, however, began to snicker and point fingers at Presbyterians when they walked down the street. When Phil Donahue flew Henry and one of his hogs up to Chicago to demonstrate the ritual on his television show, the animal got frightened by the studio lights and clammed up and made a mess, and the audience laughed. Senator William Proxmire gave the Pentagon his top Golden Fleece Award that year for its support of the research project that wasted the most tax dollars. (It beat out the one where the government

The Praying Pigs

spent $50,000 to determine that the best bait for mice was cheese.) And *Time* magazine slyly gave a senator from Tennessee its "Pork Barrel Lifetime Achievement Award" for his behind-the-scenes role in the affair.

The ridicule got so great that the General Assembly of the Presbyterian Church finally had to address the matter at its annual meeting. The leaders faced a dilemma. They couldn't deny their own heritage and discredit the speech of even the most disgusting of God's creatures, particularly since they were mentioned in the Bible.

But they found their way around the problem. After much discussion, they recommended that henceforth only officially ordained Presbyterian pastors be permitted to individually pray out loud at church services.

And the headquarters of the southern branch of the church in Atlanta came up with a slogan for the parsons to use to promote the practice. It was patterned after an old Greyhound Bus commercial and was introduced that fall as the "Relax and Leave the Praying to Us" campaign.

And because any pig-like sounds seemed to diminish all other individual out-loud prayers, many other denominations began to follow suit. While most mainstream Protestant churches now don't officially ban such individual conduct by their members, they do their best to discourage such practices—and particularly any Calvinist-type utterings.

So the ministers pray, and the people in the pews listen. It must be noted that there are some occasional lapses. A few of the older male members of some congregations are known to emit some sounds from the ancient Presbyterian language during Sabbath services.

This usually occurs during an overly long sermon, when the church is too warm. If the snores and snorts get to sounding too loud, a nudge in the ribs or a tap on the shoulder usually brings the violator around.

You should watch yourself. Any kind of individual out-loud prayers are frowned on in modern-day mainline denominations—all because of the praying pigs.

Doing the Right Thing for the Wrong Reasons

Most Christians have good intentions. Some folks even believe that a Christian is someone who feels that injustice is simply good intentions gone awry. Others claim that the definition of "do-gooder" in some dictionaries includes the word "Christian."

A great deal of Good Samaritan work is done in and on behalf of many churches. And if you become a church member, you should be prepared to "enter in," as they say. There are many possibilities such as collecting food for the homeless, donating blood, shipping used clothing to Czechoslovakia, and other charity work that will give you a warm glow. A few folk feel that donating funds to the foundation that seeks to convert the people in a French village who worship a sixty-five-foot statue of Jerry Lewis is particularly satisfying.

Within your own church, you'll find satisfaction in visiting the sick and consoling the bereaved. But you may have to put up with some wonderfully officious folk who create and run some of the worthy causes. They are often inspired by reasons other than a desire to be helpful. Some have their own agenda and are prompted by considerations that are often not readily apparent. A few are simply mountebanks.

It's best, however, not to question their motivation too closely. It's usually better to remember an old tale they tell around church campfires about how people sometimes do the right thing for the wrong reasons.

The events happened in a small midwestern town during the Great Depression. The tyranny of two small decisions set off a series of unintended, but wonderful, consequences.

The town of 1,300 was nestled between two creeks in the rolling small hills of northwest Iowa. Like its neighbors, it existed to support the people who farmed the rich black earth that many people claimed to be the most productive in all the world.

On the surface, the place was a bucolic heaven. Its citizens moved at a slow pace and lived lives that weren't used very much. They were quite a stoic lot, full of guilt and resignation, believing that if you didn't get what you wanted from the grocery store by ten o'clock on Saturday night, you probably deserved to wait until Monday morning.

Doing the Right Thing for the Wrong Reasons

There were high school basketball games during the cold winter months, and in the summer the circus came to town. Everybody knew one another and one another's business and talked to one another about it. All in all, it was a terrifically intimate kind of place, where the postmaster's daughter could send a postcard back home to her boyfriend with a "Hi Dad" scrawled on the edge next to the message.

Beneath this placid surface, however, was a deep division. The town was split between Catholic and Protestant allegiances, the Protestants being represented by the Methodists. The two sides had inherited centuries of distrust and suspicions, and the little town had two churches, two lifestyles, and two schools.

The public school was on one side of town, and the Catholic academy was across the street from the rectory, the convent, and the big brick cathedral on the other side of town. Both schools offered instruction from kindergarten through the twelfth grade. The entire collection of Catholic buildings was called Saint Anthony's, after the ancient who resisted all sorts of temptations in the desert. The name was supposed to inspire similar behavior among the modern-day members of the parish, particularly the high school kids.

There were some forty-five of them at Saint Anthony's and about a hundred at the public high school, which put both at a decided disadvantage in sports or music competitions with schools from similar-size towns in the area that had but one school—a public one. The city fathers, of course, had the good sense never to allow the two schools in the little town to compete with one another, although the freshman boys from Saint Anthony's did go over to the public school to take a manual training course because that school had lathes and band saws.

Otherwise, the two sets of youngsters didn't speak. There was no dating between Catholics and Methodists, and they held separate dances. In fact, a real antagonism existed. The Methodist kids called the Catholic kids "Mackerel Snappers" or "Catlickers," and the Catholic youngsters believed the rumor that their counterparts hid tiny pieces of meat in cupcakes and had them delivered to their lunchroom on Fridays. And they pitied the Methodist kids because they had a cross with nobody on it.

There were even occasional fistfights when the two factions ran into one another unexpectedly. It was all very stupid—but real.

The division between the kids, of course, was simply a reflection of the adult world around them. The Masonic and Knights of

The Potluck Dinner that Went Astray

Columbus lodges were across the street from one another downtown, and with the ladies it was understood that the Garden Club and P.E.O. were for the Methodists, while the Tourist Club was a Catholic enclave. The Commercial Club consisted mostly of merchants who were members of Saint Anthony's, while the Rotarians were made up of the followers of John Wesley.

The religious cleavage even extended beyond this life. The town boasted of two cemeteries—adjacent to one another to be sure, but quite separate. As far back as anyone could remember, nobody from one faith had found peace and a final resting place in the grounds of the other.

The wide chasm between the Methodists and Catholics was not unique to the little town. Some historians have maintained that the major social and political divisions in the Midwest in the first half of the twentieth century were due to the Catholic-Protestant rift.

As Iowa author Thomas J. Morain has pointed out, a big difference separated the two on such matters as repentance and the role of the clergy. The Protestants placed an emphasis on the responsibility of individuals for their own salvation. The Catholics, however, put the church in the role of a mediator between individuals and God. And for them, confession, communion, baptism, and the last rites were essential steps in salvation. The Methodists placed much less importance on the role of the sacraments, and anyhow, they said, how could Catholics be 100 percent American if they were answerable to a foreign power—the Pope in Rome?

This last one cut to the heart of the differences. To the democratic Methodists, the hierarchical structure of the Catholic church gave the "higher-ups" a dictatorial hold over their members that denied individual thought. To the Catholics, such order was necessary to preserve and nurture the faith.

So the tensions in the little town were real, although they were usually hidden behind a polite Hawkeye face. After all, there were other things to think about.

The nation was struggling to climb out of the biggest depression people had ever known. In the United States, more than thirteen million men could not find work, and more than thirty million around the world were unemployed. There was famine in Russia, and suicides in the United States were common, as business after business failed after the Wall Street crash of 1929. The farm crisis had eased off somewhat

Doing the Right Thing for the Wrong Reasons

by this time, but still one in seven farmers were continuing to lose land by foreclosure.

Yet, life was reasonably serene on the surface in the little town. President Roosevelt had just been elected to his second term, and his administration's efforts were beginning to pay off. Prices were easing up for corn and livestock. And the little kids around town had begun to buy marbles again and to find old inner tubes to fashion ammunition for rubber-gun fights.

It was therefore a bit of a shock when the Catholic-Protestant thing boiled up in a most unlikely manner. It surfaced during an election for the minor political post of county supervisor (the incumbent had died in office).

There were five county supervisors who were elected on a staggered basis. That year, the representative from the district that included the little town was to be chosen.

Political party allegiances in the rural Iowa of the time often did not follow traditional lines. Catholics sometimes voted Republican, and Protestants often marked the Democrat side of the ballot. The Board of Supervisors post was a part-time job that paid but a pittance, although it carried with it some prestige. The duties of the position included the levying of taxes and establishment of the county budget, along with the supervision of roads, the sheriff's department, and the county district court where what little malfeasance as happened in the area was dealt with.

One contender for the post was Merle McIntyre, a Republican and a Catholic. He was the heir apparent to the very successful farm implement business in town and thought that his father's money made him smart. He did have a solid grasp of the unimportant, and that was important in the local politics of the day.

But his posturing did not endear him to some people around town. His rather blustery manner and glad-handing struck people as phony, although he was careful to help the men unload a new shipment of machinery off the box cars down at the railroad depot on occasion to prove that he was just one of the boys.

Merle's wife went by the name of Mavis. They had married right out of high school. She was a sort of a flibbertigibbet who spent most of her days inventing different kinds of tea, such as onion-banana pekoe, in an attempt to make the stuff interesting.

The Potluck Dinner that Went Astray

Merle was of course Irish, like most of the members of Saint Anthony's. It was sometimes difficult to like him or any other Irishman for that reason alone, particularly on Saint Patrick's Day when people said they were so full of themselves. And Mavis, being a member of Our Lady of Knock, Division 3, of the Ladies Ancient Order of Hibernians (AOH), didn't help matters.

Merle said he was running for office to bring new ideas to an old post. In reality, the implement store had outgrown its quarters, and his dad had decided to construct a new building and big display yard on the edge of town. His son's position on the Board of Supervisors would ensure that the county road that ran by the new site would eventually be paved.

Merle's opponent was Tommy Thomas, an unlikely candidate. He had left town after graduation from high school, got a degree from Iowa State College in journalism, and had headed for Chicago and fame and fortune. He got a job at the legendary City News Bureau whose motto was "Accuracy, Accuracy, Accuracy." It was the nation's oldest training ground for cub reporters, who suffered low salaries and cranky editors, to learn their trade. He even took the guff of the curmudgeonly night editor who was known to bellow at his quaking charges: "You say your mother loves you? Check it out!"

Tommy graduated to a job at one of the dailies, but things just didn't work out. He failed to advance out of routine reportorial duties and began to drink. Soon he became so familiar with a particular bar stool at the working-class tavern he frequented that his fellow habitues installed a plaque with his name on it on the armrest of the stool.

He was a thoughtful guy, though, plying his lady companions with a lot of booze so they would have an excuse the next morning. His nights—and later days—were filled with seamed silk stockings, and when he was in his cups he would announce to one and all that his favorite band was Phil Spitalny and His All-Girl Orchestra, featuring "Evelyn and Her Magic Violin." And it was his intention, he would holler, to have his way with all of them!

Tommy's hangovers eventually got so bad, however, that he could not handle the sound of someone raking leaves, let alone the clacking of his typewriter, and he began to realize that he was scrambling to hang on to a spinning world. He finally had to stop the boozing because he kept waking up across the state line in Indiana with a boisterous female who worked in one of the steel mills in Gary. On such

Doing the Right Thing for the Wrong Reasons

mornings, he developed such a hankering for popcorn that he could have devoured the whole state of Iowa.

So after a drying-out period in Des Moines, Tommy went home to where he could find a leash on life. Folks said he cleaned up real good.

He got a low-paying job as the only employee of the local weekly newspaper where he served as a reporter-ad salesman-typesetter. He began to go out with an old high school classmate who was a waitress at the snack counter at the bowling alley. His parents were Methodist, and he even went back to church. And when Tommy was approached by the Democrats to run for the Board of Supervisors, he agreed. He said that, like Saul on the way to Tarsus, he had received a signal—in his case to run for office to help the downtrodden.

In reality he hated folderol, bombast, braggadocio—and Merle McIntyre, ever since he had been beaten up by him in a fight in high school. And if the truth was known, the party leaders picked Tommy because he was the only person they could find to run for what had always been a Republican seat.

So the battle was joined between those not-so-honorable men, one a scheming scoundrel and the other a reformed drunk. Each had his own private motivation, which he tried to hide from his supporters, but in a small town there are few secrets. Most people figured it all out eventually.

The candidates' followers were split along religious lines with the sort-of conservative Catholics for Merle and the sort-of liberal Methodists for Tommy. Both of the new politicians were thirty-one years-old, the youngest contenders ever for the office.

Neither man was an effective speaker, on or off the campaign trail. Merle was full of gallimaufry and undigested thought. He usually settled into one theme in his campaign speeches, concentrating (Bill Harley said) "on the constant reiteration of the forever unclear." If questioned by a listener, he resorted to his imitation of Lawrence Welk, who was becoming popular in those parts. His "uh one, an'uh two" fairly convulsed his audiences.

Tommy wasn't much better. He had a tendency to lapse into soggy sentimentality. And although his speeches were short, he rambled a lot. This had one positive effect: People listened closely because they didn't know where he was going.

Down at the pool hall, the town wag, Ray Wilberdang, said that Tommy's speeches reminded him of the cross-eyed discus thrower at

The Potluck Dinner that Went Astray

the track meet. He didn't toss it very far, but the people who were watching sure did pay attention when he cranked up to throw the thing!

'Course, Ray was Catholic.

There weren't really any issues to haggle about, and both candidates seldom touched the minds of those they addressed. People wanted the nationwide depression to be over and prosperity to return, but the County Board of Supervisors didn't have much influence over that.

Folks did want the county to do something about the bums who had been bothering everyone for the last few years. The hobos showed up at the back door of the homes of many of the housewives in town, asking for a handout. The good matrons adopted a "mercy me and hide the silver" attitude about the whole thing, but in typical Iowa fashion, hardly any of the ne'er-do-wells were refused. Some said that the vagrants then drew the secret sign of a smiling cat on the house somewhere, which alerted their fellow migrants that the housewife inside was kind and this was a good place to cadge a meal.

The bums had been pestering the ladies so much that they had become a nuisance. When they weren't skulking through the alleys of the town, they camped in a sort of shantytown across the railroad tracks beside one of the creeks. The Town Council couldn't do anything about the collection of cardboard and wooden packing boxes that was such an eyesore, because it was on land owned by the county. So it was up to the Board of Supervisors.

Merle was seeking an edge in the contest and seized on the circumstance. In a canny tactic, he decided to preempt his liberal opponent by announcing that he and the Republican party were establishing a homeless shelter downtown in a vacant automobile showroom, which they borrowed from a lawyer in town. They got some donated cots and started to rig up some showers, and the CYO kids from Saint Anthony's used some of their funds to provide pillows and blankets. Merle said that if he were elected, he'd see to it that the county would take over the responsibility for the place.

This maneuver caused a great deal of consternation in the ranks of the Democrats, and after mulling it over and huddling with his advisors for two days, Tommy came up with his own plan. He would establish a soup kitchen for the bums. After all, their begging for food was *really* the problem. And just to prove that the Democrats were

Doing the Right Thing for the Wrong Reasons

tolerant and could put partisan politics aside for the good of the community, Tommy got an O.K. from the lawyer to establish the food dispensary in the same automobile showroom.

The cynics down at the pool hall said it could hardly have been otherwise; the lawyer was a resolutely nonpartisan hack who sought business from everyone, and prudent Iowans of either political or religious persuasion wouldn't have countenanced the extravagance of using two buildings when one would do. And anyhow, there wasn't another empty building on Main Street.

So the Democrats got the Epworth League kids from the Methodist church to buy some big pots and pans, and they began to rig up a makeshift kitchen in the back of the building. Tommy said that if he was elected, he'd see to it that the county would take over the responsibility for the operation.

During the remodeling phase, the two sides had to coordinate their plumbing activities. And so the chairman of the local Republican party (a member of the Knights of Columbus) and the chairman of the Democrat party (a Mason) began to have some brief conversations. And when it came time to work out the hourly schedules for the operation of the place, the ladies from the Methodist Ladies Aid, who were doing the soup, were obliged to make common cause with the ladies from the Society of the Sacred Heart, who were going to hand out the towels and blankets. Mind you, at first it was all nods and gestures, but eventually some dialogue began to take place.

After two weeks of labor and planning, the establishment was ready to open. No one could come up with a name that wouldn't offend somebody, so it remained nameless. But everybody was in an anticipatory mood. The ladies stood poised behind their respective tables with soup ladles and bars of soap at the ready. And on a beautiful spring day, they opened the doors.

The problem was, no bums showed up. The organizers sent the local depot agent of the Illinois Central Railroad down to the shantytown to make sure that the vagabonds knew about the place, but those boys were having none of it. As "Knights of the Road," the hobos valued their independence and "didn't want no institutional handouts—thank you very much." Individual begging and camping out was part of the mystique of a wandering life of riding the rails.

So as the days passed, the place started to become an embarrassment for everyone—Catholics, Republicans, Democrats, Methodists.

The Potluck Dinner that Went Astray

But the ladies continued to staff it every day in the hope that some down-on-their-luck person would come through the doors.

Meanwhile, the political campaign proceeded apace. The two candidates personally confronted one another on only one occasion—and that wasn't much of a meeting.

They agreed to debate at the Pilot Rock Plowing Contest south of town on an April Saturday. The event was held on a farmer's field near a mammoth boulder that had been deposited by a glacier centuries ago and used as a landmark in pioneer days.

The contest was an all-day affair, during which some farmers competed with one another to see who could plow the most land in a given time. Temporary lunch stands were set up and run by the two churches. And most people in the area made a day of it. The ladies came because they had some social business to attend to, and the husbands who weren't entering the competition came because they simply wanted a day off from hard labor. It was sort of satisfying to watch someone else work for a change.

Merle and Tommy and their supporters showed up and established camps at each end of a field about fifty yards from one another. What ensued came to be known later as the "Battle of the Bands," for both candidates had brought their entertainment with them.

Merle's group was a three-piece country-western organization that only knew the three basic chords, but that was okay; the songs they played seldom required more than four, and they could sometimes fake the extra one. The band was installed on the back of a big flatbed truck. Merle handed out caps (said to be new) with "Allis Chalmers" written on them. In a not-too-subtle dig at his opponent, he had his band play what has since become the country classic, "How Can I Miss You, When You Won't Go Away?"

Across the field, Tommy (with more limited funds) mounted his aggregation on the back of a pickup truck. His group consisted of a rather stout friend of his mother's, Mrs. Neva Custer, a mezzo soprano who was accompanied on the accordion by Mrs. Vera Bartle. Mrs. Custer favored the crowd with semiclassical selections from the turn of the century, including "Just a Wearyin' for You" and "Ah! Sweet Mystery of Life (at Last I've Found You)." After some campaign workers helped the ladies down, Tommy would climb aboard to talk to those who gathered round.

Doing the Right Thing for the Wrong Reasons

The crowd shifted back and forth between the two candidates, who alternated music with pleas for support. The potential voters shuffled from one location to the other, moving in accord as almost one entity. To the kids who had climbed up Pilot Rock to watch the spectacle, it looked like one big beast with hundreds of legs moving first from one side and then to the other side of the field!

The debate was pretty much a dialogue of the deaf. Neither candidate could hear one another, and neither man even acknowledged the presence of the other.

The election was held about three weeks later. Ray, down at the pool hall, said that Tommy had about as much chance as a one-legged man in a butt-kicking contest.

'Course, Ray was Catholic.

In the end, Tommy lost—big. A lot of the men around town didn't quite trust him, but not because of his past—of that they were envious. No, he wasn't one of them; he didn't really work for a living. They thought he should give up the newspaper writing and get a real job. The ladies said that Merle won because he had a farmer's tan and more hair on his arms.

In spite of the fact that there were no patrons, the shelter-soup kitchen remained open while Merle tried to get the O.K. for its support and continued operation on the supervisors' meeting agenda. Neither side—Republican nor Democrat—wanted its participation to be seen as a political expedient. What was really at stake, of course, was Catholic-Methodist pride. Neither wanted to be the first to give it up.

But as the ladies lost interest in showing up every day, the job fell more and more to the CYO and Epworth League kids. And both groups started to eye one another with increasing interest from their positions at their respective tables.

Some hope for the usefulness of the place came from an unexpected source: the strikes and labor stoppages at the meat-packing plants in Sioux City thirty miles away. The unrest there was agitated by the extreme left of the labor movement in the United States, the IWW (International Workers of the World)—the "Wobblies," as they were called. They had made the city a "western" rallying point at this stage of the Depression, and out-of-work men poured into it to support the striking workers. Hearing about the shelter-soup kitchen, they grabbed the first freight train to the little town and nearly overwhelmed the facility.

The Potluck Dinner that Went Astray

The Catholic and Methodist kids who were manning the place were in a state of shock. They found themselves helping not good old professional American hobos, but rather foreign-looking, unkempt men with accents who had strange-sounding names and argued constantly at the top of their lungs in a decidedly un-Iowa way. The youngsters began to exchange knowing glances among themselves and to develop a sort of unified "at least we're not like them" attitude.

The Wobblies only stayed a week or so, however, before they moved on to a new western gathering point in Salt Lake City. By that time, Merle had got the Board of Supervisors to consider taking over the operation of the place. But they turned his proposal down by a 4 to 1 vote, saying they weren't about to spend county money to shelter and feed assorted communists, radicals, and anarchists!

That was pretty much the last straw. Even the kids began to lose their enthusiasm for the project, and staffing the empty facility began to become a big problem. Finally, Father Shaughnessy of Saint Anthony's and Reverend Millbank of the Methodist church had to step in.

The two had been studiously avoiding the place—and one another. Neither had wanted to be accused of even unofficially condoning the mixing of religion and politics. In point of fact, neither had ever really spoken to the other since they had been in town, each fearing that their parishioners would accuse them of consorting with the "enemy."

But something had to be done, and the two religious professionals began to talk about schedules and upkeep on the telephone, which graduated over time to an inspection of the premises and some formal meetings there. They even agreed on a name for the place: "The Loaves, Fishes, and Cots"—but that didn't help attendance. Finally, the two clerics decided that the place should be closed, and it was.

By that time, a sort of grudging respect for one another had begun to develop. When a Methodist lad approached them about the two churches sponsoring a monthly community dance at the municipal building so the kids would have something to do that summer, they promised to think it over. The two clergymen finally gave their permission, even though they knew that the reason for the request was that the Protestant kid had a crush on a Catholic girl.

And so for the first time that anyone could remember, a social event was held for the young people of the two religions in the community. The two clerics were on hand to ensure the peace, and the adults around town marveled at the occasion!

Doing the Right Thing for the Wrong Reasons

Well, wouldn't you know, this co-religious dance led to the eventual integration of Boy Scout Troop #114, which had previously been a Methodist preserve, and the establishment that winter of a community ice-skating rink as a cooperative venture of the KCs and the Masons. Old-timers really shook their heads, however, when they heard that the wife of the choir director of the Methodist Church was sending her nine-year-old to Sister Mary Cecilia at Saint Anthony's for piano lessons.

She was doing so, she said, because the nun was the best piano teacher in town.

The next year someone suggested that the churches sponsor an ecumenical carol fest to kick off the Christmas season. The only place big enough to hold it was Saint Anthony's, and the event would require some planning. So the two religious leaders and their choir directors met there one afternoon. It was the first time the rather stodgy Methodist minister had ever been in the Catholic church, and after working out the logistics, they all repaired to the priest's study in the rectory to plan the music. After the carols had been chosen and the music directors had gone, the two pastors lapsed into a comfortable silence in the warmth of the room.

The priest offered his compatriot a glass of sherry to celebrate the successful planning of the event. Not wanting to offend, the minister accepted, even though he hadn't touched spirits since his college days. The two got to reminiscing about the events of the past two years, and particularly about Merle and Tommy's old shelter-soup kitchen and how it had come to be.

The Reverend Millbank was moved to observe how he was often amazed about how people sometimes did the right thing for the wrong reasons, such as the time he had stayed in the college library on a Friday night because he called too late to get a date.

Father Shaughnessy murmured an assent, confessing that, as a child, he had once gone to Mass three times one Sunday morning in order to get enough points to beat out his best friend for a shiny medal.

And then they both contemplated the pattern that the fading sunlight made on the floor through the stained-glass windows, as the big clock in the corner ticked away.

The Potluck Dinner that Went Astray

The moment called for another glass, and the two continued their cozy chat, even regaling one another with old seminary stories. When they parted, it was with increased respect—and near friendship.

The day had other salutary effects. When the usually less-than-amorous Reverend Millbank arrived home, he had a bit of a bounce in his step. He was, well, frisky—so much so that as he passed his wife peeling potatoes for supper at the kitchen sink, he gave her a little pat on the rear end. And just that night after another glass of wine at dinner, Father Shaughnessy had his first good night's sleep in weeks.

Things got even better. Over the years, the Catholics and Methodists in the little town became more tolerant of one another and cooperated on many things for the good of the community. They even began to gossip. The carol fest is now in its fifty-third year, but the two clerics have, of course, long since gone to their reward. Their successors, however, even preside over an occasional mixed marriage of a Catholic and a Methodist, and few eyebrows are raised around town.

Saint Andrew's Academy was closed in the 1960s, and the kids of both religions now attend a brand new consolidated public school in the center of the community. It offers a much broader curriculum than either one could have ever afforded alone. Although Saint Andrew's demise was more a matter of economics than ecumenism, those with long memories date the beginning of its closure to Tommy and Merle and the soup kitchen-shelter.

Down at the pool hall, Ray still holds forth. When prompted, he says that this thing about doing the right thing for the wrong reason reminds him that he joined the Navy three months before Pearl Harbor because his girlfriend said he'd look good in blue.

'Course, Ray's still Catholic.

Today, both the Methodists and Catholics use the tale of the little town to remind everyone that you shouldn't question the motives of your fellow human beings when it comes to doing good deeds. God somehow makes it come out all right.

And people should probably know that Merle did get the county road paved in front of the new implement store and inherited the business. And Tommy married his waitress friend and eventually became the editor-owner of the paper. They're both great-grandfathers now and retired, and they occasionally have a beer together down at the pool hall.

Washed in the Blood of the Lamb

Few ministers of mainstream denominations lure people into their fold with promises of salvation and redemption. Unlike the Fundamentalists and Mormons, mainline pastors don't usually proselytize. And they certainly don't indulge in faith healing.

These precepts became a sort of unofficial posture of many denominations in the late nineteenth century due to an incident that happened in a small town in Iowa. There, a church found that it is best to do nothing and wait patiently for people to become members of their own free will *and* to avoid any laying on of hands.

The little town of Hastings was founded in 1871, largely by Civil War veterans who were heading west but stopped when they reached the gentle contours and rich black earth of the Corn State. Many of them were from the South and brought their Baptist religion with them. One of the first things they did after they founded the little village was to erect a church.

They wrested the establishment of the county seat away from an already growing hamlet called Highmore, some twelve miles to the west, and laid out the place in the classical Roman grid, with streets crisscrossing in the orderly rectangular manner. The farm economy was booming right after the war, and in spite of grasshopper plagues, prairie fires, and an occasional tornado, the village grew.

The Illinois Central Railroad took the farmers' crops and livestock to bigger markets, and by the late 1880s, the town boasted of two banks, two dry goods stores, Larson's Confectionery (where you could get a plate of ice cream), and Elmer's Tonsorial Parlor and Dental Emporium. The latter was the oldest barbershop in town and a gathering place for the village loafers who could there speculate about "what coulda', what woulda', and what shoulda' happened."

Elmer had some competition from "The Only Barbershop under the Sidewalk in the World: Chas. McAlaster Prop." Mr. McAlaster had come to town in 1885 and set up shop in the basement under one bank, and no polite Iowan ever questioned the claim on the big sign that he put up at the top of the stairs.

The Potluck Dinner that Went Astray

There was also a modern livery stable with a blacksmith, an implement store that carried plows and tools, a hatchery, and two saloons—one downtown between the feed store and the *Hastings Chronicle,* and one on the way out of town called the Eastside Tavern. The streets were dusty and wouldn't be paved for another twenty-five years, but altogether about 950 people called Hastings home.

Most of the businesses were arranged around the courthouse square, where an American version of an Egyptian funeral temple had been proudly erected in 1896 to serve as the legal and governmental headquarters of O'Brien County. It was something to see!

The town had resisted an attempt by Highmore two years previous to steal the county seat back. Some of the lads from that town, "emboldened by strong spirits" (according to the story in the *Chronicle*), snuck into town one night and carried off the safe with all the county records from the old wooden building that served at that time as the courthouse. An alarm was raised, but the boys got away. They weren't going to give it back, they said; but in the sober light of morning, wiser heads prevailed, and the safe was eventually returned intact.

Just to ensure that such an event wouldn't recur, the town council got the voters in the county to authorize the construction of the concrete, temple-like structure with two palm-front columns flanking the entrance steps. It was an imposing edifice for the time, and its Egyptian motif added a touch of cosmopolitanism to the town. In addition, there were hitching posts all around the square and even a little gazebo bandstand on the courthouse grounds.

Much of the prosperity of the village was due to the guys in the Commercial Club, most of whom were also members of the Hastings Volunteer Fireman's Association and Rescue Company. The Commercial Club worked diligently to bring new ventures to town and encourage trade. At one of its monthly meetings, someone mentioned that Highmore was getting another railroad through town, along with a big new hotel and a flour mill, and was making noises about appropriating the county seat again—this time legally.

So the group took stock. What did Highmore have to offer the voters of the county that Hastings did not? As they ticked off the comparisons, one thing stood out. Highmore had three churches, and Hastings had but one—the original Baptist structure on the south side of the courthouse square. Not that a church brought much money or

Washed in the Blood of the Lamb

business into town, but such things made a place—well—more respectable.

The Baptist church was just struggling along, however, with an aging and a sort of lackadaisical congregation. Another church might sink it for good. On the other hand, said one of the bankers, some competition might be salutary.

He reminded the club that when the community was first founded, it couldn't support one lawyer. When another one came to town, both prospered because everybody began suing everybody else. Eventually, there were three of them, and their presence was one reason Hastings was still the county seat.

So the club decided to get another church. But what kind? It had to be unique or different, and as they went through the possibilities, they began to despair.

Iowa was already swarming with Methodists. The Congregationalists were anarchists. They had no authority above them, so who could control them? The pope was the anti-Christ, so Catholics were out. And with the Lutherans, you couldn't be sure what language you would get. The little town of Cedar River, 21 miles to the south, with a population of only 700, had three Lutheran churches: Danish, Swedish, and Norwegian. They were all across the street from one another, and each held services in its native tongue. The Anglicans had Thirty-Nine Articles, and the Jews had 613 Commandments of Faith, and everybody agreed that both numbers were simply too many for rural Iowans to remember and live up to.

No one knew much about the Presbyterians, but somebody said he'd heard that they believed in only one statement. There wasn't a church of that denomination within 200 miles, at least; and because nobody could come up with any reason not to invite them to come to town, it was settled. The feed store owner said he'd donate a lot on the north side of the square for them to build a church on.

Upon investigation, the group found that there were some German Presbyterian churches across the state around Dubuque and even a theological school. But the organization rejected petitioning it, largely because anyone from there would be—well—too German. So, after some more discreet inquiries as to where else to write, the president of the club sent off a letter to the Board of Home Missions of the Presbyterian Church in Philadelphia, describing Hastings and its spiritual needs.

The Potluck Dinner that Went Astray

There were sinners out here on the prairie, he said. And after about three months, the club got a letter back saying that the Presbyterian Church would be delighted to help start up a church in Hastings, Iowa.

What the good burghers didn't know was that the denomination was in an unholy uproar, largely over the Westminster Confession of Faith. This was the basic belief of the church and the statement of faith at the time.

But in a day when people were arguing over the teachings of evolution in the schools and new archaeological discoveries were being made in the Holy Land that shed new light on the Bible, many Presbyterians were agitating for a revision of "The Westminster." They were especially anxious to modify Chapter Three of the Confession called "Of God's Eternal Decree," which addressed the issue of predestination.

This staunch statement said that God had predestined those intended for salvation—and only a few had been so elected. This was the very heart of strict Calvinism, but it seemed to encourage a sort of fatalism and a *que sera, sera* attitude in people. I mean, if you had no way to work toward your own salvation, what was the point of attending all those blasted committee meetings? At the least, it put a crimp in the missionary work of the church, because it was difficult to recruit people to an uncertain future.

The liberal wing of the Presbyterian church was intent on rectifying this hindrance and promoted the notion that every sinner could gain salvation. The argument was to rage for several years, with Mark Twain poking fun at what he called "Presbyterian Preforeordestination." And in spite of a modification of the Westminster in 1903 and a new Confession in 1967, the issue has never been really satisfactorily resolved within that denomination.

All of this, of course, was foreign to the Commercial Club of Hastings. Presbyterianism was essentially an East Coast religion at the time and had just established a toehold in eastern Iowa. Its internal theological squabbles had not reached the prairies of the western part of the state. So, blissfully unaware of the argument, the pragmatic Hawkeyes prepared to greet the new parson they had petitioned for.

When he stepped off the afternoon train from Sioux City, they were taken back a bit by his youth. The Board of Home Missions had decided to send one, A. P. Cooper, who was fresh out of the Western

Washed in the Blood of the Lamb

Theological Seminary in Pittsburgh, Pennsylvania, for they weren't about to possibly waste an experienced hand in a hotbed of Methodists and Lutherans in the really far "out West." He was a gangly fellow with (as Louise Cook put it) "legs from here to tomorrow." Even though he was young, he was a bona fide graduate of a three-year program and not "field educated" by a pastor/teacher.

Although the good Reverend Cooper had, of course, sworn to the Westminster as a part of the requirements of his profession, he wasn't quite yet sure what he really believed. So he did the prudent Presbyterian thing and kept his mouth shut about the whole predestination hassle.

After looking over the building lot and noting the paucity of trees and lumber in town, he sent a request back to the Board of Church Erections, and in due time a precut church arrived from New York. It was speedily put up, and although its steeple was not as tall as that of the Baptist church across the square, this seemed somehow to be altogether proper, for it was befitting of the new kid in town and the inherent modesty of the denomination.

The New England-style white clapboard edifice, which had the traditional two side aisles (Design No. 2), opened its doors for worship to a packed house on a scorchingly hot Sunday morning in August of 1891. A lot of the town folk came out just to see what it was like inside. And they liked it.

The minister of the Baptist church warmly welcomed his brother-in-Christ, and he and the Reverend Cooper got along just fine. The Baptist parson was a tired, elderly veteran who was in his twentieth year of service to the community. He had seen it all and welcomed another religious choice for the people of the village. He now had someone to alternate with on the religious civic duties such as blessing cornerstones or conducting the baccalaureate services at the new high school every spring.

The two ministers even worked out a relief fund accommodation, with the Baptists concentrating on farm families and the Presbyterians doling out their benevolence in town. Both churches held their main services at 11:00 A.M. on Sundays, and the Dew Drop Inn Cafe did a good business in chicken dinners afterwards.

Of course, there was an inevitable erosion in the membership of the Baptist church. When people died, it was hard to replace them, for many newcomers to town opted for the lanky young man's sermons at

The Potluck Dinner that Went Astray

the Presbyterian church, and Reverend Cooper was also particularly adept at combing the town's byways for unchurched people. He even landed the town drunk and the community's professional virgin.

There were no outright defections from the Baptists, however, and so the religious life of the village prospered in peace. The Commercial Club congratulated itself on its sagacity, the night watchman reported to the town council a slight decrease in arrests for drunkenness, business was increasing in spite of a nationwide recession, and everyone seemed happy.

Everyone that is, except Lawyer Nugent. Mr. Nugent was the original attorney in town and a leader in the Baptist church. Although he had profited from the appearance in town of a second and eventually a third lawyer, he still resented their presence, and lately he had been chafing at the decline in the membership of his church. When the Baptist parson died suddenly, under the leadership of Lawyer Nugent, the congregation replaced him with a fortyish go-getter from Arkansas.

The fellow was probably doomed before he even got into town. When word got around that his last name was Moley, the wags who hung around Elmer's immediately tagged him with a first-name nickname "Holy."

And he appeared to live up to the name. He blew into Hastings with a sanctified look, a perpetual smile on his face, and an arm-twisting technique of greeting people.

Moley was a rather pompous, blustering fellow with charisma to spare. His portly frame sported a supposedly gold watch fob across his vest. He explained to anyone who asked that it had been presented to him by members of his previous congregation in honor of his first year with them. There seemed to be more than a hint in that, and as he had served his previous church for some five years, everyone in his new congregation was afraid to ask what other gifts had been bestowed on him during that time, lest they become similarly responsible.

The Reverend Moley set about restoring the dominance of the Baptists in town by aggressively preaching hellfire and brimstone, and he was so effective at it that he scared the bejesus out of everybody. His description of Satan and the fiery furnace set youngsters wailing. And he pounded the Bible and the pulpit with a fervor that had never been seen in those parts.

Washed in the Blood of the Lamb

Some of his sermons were rambling, however, and many were so tangled up in convoluted syntax that they became unintentionally humorous. His congregation sometimes had to struggle to follow the twists and turns of his continuing interest in Bathsheba, and on more than one Sunday, they left the church in a rather befuddled state. Some folks just stopped going, figuring they didn't need more confusion in their lives.

The Reverend Moley was anything but insensitive to his flock, however, and as attendance continued to dwindle, he started to resort to more drastic measures to hold his congregation. He began to simplify his sermons and to warn of the impending apocalypse and the need for repentance. He started to punctuate his sermons with a directive to "Gimme an Amen!" usually after a particularly soaring bit of evangelistic rhetoric, thereby seeking instant endorsement for his remarks.

And after a prayerful meeting with Lawyer Nugent one night, he came up with the ultimate scheme. He would get new members by using the same contingency principles that many attorneys used.

The deal was that if you joined, he'd get you into heaven. If you didn't make it, your name would be erased from the rolls and your offerings returned.

Even the dolts around town saw the fallacy in that offer, for the good Reverend Moley couldn't prove that he had personally seen to it that Saint Peter had welcomed even one of his past parishioners. So when people still resisted coming out on Sundays, he resorted to a practice he had used earlier in his career: faith healing.

He began to work it into the Sunday morning services more in desperation than anything else, and although there were some skeptics, he appeared to have a little success. Sister Wackler's rheumatism "seemed some better," she said, after he laid on the hands one Sabbath; and little Jimmy Conklin got over his cough. So Moley began to spend more time in the ritual, and he had Lawyer Nugent and others spread the word around town that he was in the healing business.

Across the square, young Reverend Cooper kept his own counsel and went about his business in a quiet manner, and his congregation grew at a slow but steady pace. He said nothing, did nothing, and promised nothing—in a good Presbyterian manner.

The Potluck Dinner that Went Astray

Now Reverend Moley had inherited a number of characters when he took over the First Baptist Church in Hastings. One of his members was known behind her back by the boys at Elmer's as "she of the bodacious ta-tas."

Her Christian name was Myrtle Pringle, and she ran the hatchery and was the bass drummer in the Hastings Ladies Cornet Band. She was also a "maiden lady," as unmarried women were called in those days. She was a spinster simply because most men around town were afraid of her. Her formidable bosoms were equal to the task of supporting a craniumful of opinions, which she was not loathe to share, and she possessed a healthy dose of skepticism when it came to her new Baptist minister.

As Moley's promises of salvation became more pronounced and his faith-healing tendencies more prevalent, Myrtle became more dubious. She also attracted a few followers. Things reached a climax one Sunday morning when Reverend Moley called forth those who were afflicted to come to the altar and be cured.

Only one person came forward: Marvin the Mutterer, a mentally handicapped lad who had been a town fixture for nearly eighteen years. Abandoned by his parents when they moved on west, he lived in a little room at the back of the feed store and earned his keep by sweeping out the place. He did no one any harm and was a gentle soul, full of compassion for a brood of cats he took care of to keep the mice away from the grain.

He had somehow heard of the new Baptist pastor's healing powers and promises, and his muddled mind evidently decided to take him up on them. Although he had never before set foot in any church, something in his twisted logic led him to think that there was hope in what the boys down at Elmer's scornfully called "Moley's Miracles." He was there, then, on that fateful Sunday, and he shambled forth when the minister called. Reverend Moley had seen the fellow around town, knew something of his history, and was delighted. After all, if on the next day Marvin accidently put together even one coherent sentence, he could claim it was the result of his healing powers.

The congregation was abuzz with excitement! Moley prayed a long prayer, thanking God for Marvin and afflicted people everywhere. Then, placing his hand on the boy's forehead, he rapidly intoned in a loud, sing-song fashion:

Washed in the Blood of the Lamb

"Do you believe? (answer 'Yes I do')."
"Do you love Jesus? (answer 'Yes I do')."
"Have you been washed in the blood of the Lamb?"

Well now! The congregation's shouts of "amen!" and "hallelujah!" came to a halt. No one had heard that question before. Even in a farm community, most people couldn't imagine such a thing!

And it was the last straw for Myrtle Pringle. She was outraged at Moley's exploitation of Marvin and even more at the last question, which she found revolting, and not to put too fine a point on it, repugnant. Bolting to her feet in disgust, she marched past the astonished preacher, up the aisle, and out of the church. With her protuberances leading the way, she swept like a dreadnought across the little town square with seven or eight of her sympathizers following in her wake.

With skirts swirling in the dust, they barreled past the incredulous eyes of the town's young blades who gathered on the steps of the little courthouse every Sunday morning to wait for the churches to get out so the downtown tavern could open. Two of them were nephews of a fellow who had been kicked out of the Baptist church three years previous for taking advantage of a widow lady in the choir loft late one night. When they saw where Myrtle and her little band were headed, one of them shouted, "Good on ya, ol' girl!"

The group got to the Presbyterian church just as young Reverend Cooper was beginning the benediction. Seeing them arrive in the back and sensing the reason, the good parson sequed into an impromptu but modest prayer of praise and thanksgiving. But when his congregation turned around and saw Myrtle and her flock, they say the shouts of the Presbyterian version of "hallelujah"—"alleluia"—could be heard clear over in Polk County. Reverend Moley left town a few weeks later.

The word of the incident spread, of course, and Presbyterian ministers throughout the land took it as an omen and a lesson. The message was: "Don't do or promise anything, and God will reward you. And don't bring up that predestination thing. And for heaven's sake, don't do any laying on of the hands!" They've been following those tenants ever since.

And the word spread even beyond that denomination. Today you usually won't find promises and proselytizing in Methodist, Lutheran, United Church of Christ, or other mainstream Protestant denominations—and certainly no faith healing. These churches just sit and wait

The Potluck Dinner that Went Astray

for new members, for most have harkened to the message from the little town in Iowa and curtailed their evangelical zeal, and with it—some say—their vigor. Pity.

And oh yes, Lawyer Nugent felt so bad about the whole deal that he took Marvin under his wing and taught him how to sort-of read and write. The lad joined the Baptist church a few years later, and when he was forty-five years-old, someone else taught him how to play "America the Beautiful" on the harmonica. So maybe there was something to "Moley's Miracles" after all.

Cousin Emma and the Great Bicycle Rebellion

The little town of Highmore, Iowa, was nestled on the banks of the Floyd River about twelve miles from the village of Hastings of "Washed in the Blood of the Lamb" fame. In fact, it had been that town's rival for the county seat. Both towns were booming in the early 1900s, as the good black earth of the Hawkeye State provided prosperity for its hardworking citizens. But, . . .

The Reverend Doctor Bushnell was in a dither, and it was of his own doing. He knew that one should never tell a Christian woman what not to do nor try to discourage her from a course of action. It just makes her more determined.

Many years before, seminary professors had warned him and other would-be ministers of this phenomenom, but he had unaccountably forgotten the advice. Now he was paying for it.

Reverend Bushnell and the Grace Methodist Episcopal Church of Highmore were being dragged kicking and screaming into the twentieth century. What had started out as a small protest about an insignificant contraption had gradually grown into some strong movements for social and political change.

The parson was unprepared for such actions. He had placidly ministered to his congregation for more than twenty-five years. This was an unheard-of time in one place for a Wesleyan parson.

He had recently persuaded his flock to erect a fine new brick structure, which looked out at the community from a prominent position at the end of Main Street. He had maintained—even slightly increased—the church membership over the years.

But as his period of service had lengthened, so had his resistance to change. Some of the younger menfolk in the congregation said he was like the ladies' bloomers on a windy clothesline; although there was a lot of movement, they pretty much stayed in the same place.

The minister had originally been assigned to the Highmore church by a district superintendent who thought Bushnell had promise and would "fit in." And he did.

The Potluck Dinner that Went Astray

He was a passable (if uninspired) preacher, for his sermons were usually the result of some of the greatest research jobs in history. There was seldom an original idea in any of them. And he was a bit long-winded, too. Some members of the Ladies Aid complained that he could pray a whole bowl of mashed potatoes cold, just asking the blessing.

But he was good at combating all kinds of sin. From his pulpit the Reverend periodically inveighed against the more noncontroversial transgressions such as blasphemy and profanity, gambling and lotteries, theater-going, card-playing, dancing, and drinking.

He was often joined in such attacks by the pastor of the other Protestant denomination in town—the German Lutherans—and occasionally by the priest of the little Catholic church that the guys down at the saloons called the Church of the Immaculate Rejection, because of its small membership.

So although all three pastors justified their existence by differences in theological emphases and ecclesiastical organization, they shared a common perspective on morality. They were for it.

And with such support, the Reverend Doctor Bushnell had led a comfortable life. But now as he looked forward to retirement, his stick-in-the-mud tranquility was being threatened. And it was all the fault of Emma Dockendorf.

He had known Emma for most of her life as a rather devout Christian young lady. Normally a quiet woman with a somewhat sultry look and a full figure, she had seemingly been content to bloom softly where she had been planted. But in the past few years she had become trouble.

And to add to the problem, she was family—a second cousin, but still she was family.

And she had developed a burr under her butt. She had become an agitator and a pest. The good parson was annoyed. A good day was when Cousin Emma stayed home.

Emma had not always been this way. She had entered the grown-up world after her graduation with the first class from Highmore High in 1888, but the future did not offer many options for a young lady in those days.

She could have become a nurse, but she had rejected that as being "too messy." Perhaps she could have become a teacher, but that

Cousin Emma and the Great Bicycle Rebellion

required some more formal study and tests and certification, and she was tired of traditional schooling at the time. And a shop clerk was not quite respectable for a person of her standing as a high school graduate. So like many of her classmates, she had opted for the life of a refined young lady while awaiting a husband.

The young females of the day were occupied with good works, embroidery, and elaborate etiquettes. Their fathers had wrested a living out of the land, working from "can't see to can't see," and were now prospering. So as the town grew and became less countryfied, their daughters attended club and church meetings, cultivated ladylike manners, started a hope chest, gossiped, and shopped downtown most every day. Their tolerant fathers joked that if the girls continued in this manner, they would have to erect a Tomb of the Unknown Shopper in someone's honor at the local cemetery.

Central to the starched pomposity of the period, of course, was the idea that fathers and other men ran the world, and women were but spectators in the hubbub of life. And most of the young ladies encouraged that attitude, finding it pleasant to be put on a pedestal.

If men shaped life, however, women also had a duty. The male of the species—on his own own—would never get beyond a jungle-inspired fight for material possessions. Nietzsche had summed up the prevailing attitude in 1887 by noting that "the purpose of all civilization is to convert man, a beast of prey, into a tame—and domestic—animal."

By civilizing men (according to the supporting theory), women (while not directly holding power by having the right to vote) could control the persons who did.

But to do so meant further self-improvement. And so Cousin Emma had set out to do just that on an informal basis, as she waited for cupid's arrow to strike.

With two of her friends, she formed the I.O. of O.G. As one of the hamlet's weekly newspapers reported,

> *A number of young ladies of the town met at the home of Miss Emma on Thursday evening last to form a young females reading circle, as well as for mutual improvement in literary matters. They call themselves "The Independent Order of Odd Girls" or the I.O. of O.G., but they want it distinctly understood that the initials do not mean the Independent Order of Old Girls, as they do not wish to claim that honor yet.*

The Potluck Dinner that Went Astray

Emma turned down the presidency of the group, but saw to it that two of her friends were elected officers in the organization. Famy B. Futter was chosen vice-president, and Luta Peterson was elected critic.

Famy was a pudgy young lady whose father owned the Highmore Greenhouse and Flower Shoppe. The boys around town said she was so well-watered that when she fell down one day she rocked herself to sleep trying to get up.

And then there was her chest. One of her former classmates, who was now a brakeman on the Illinois Central Railroad, said that she had the greatest observation platform he had ever seen.

On the other hand, Luta was a 6'1" beanpole with a high-pitched voice that rose even higher when she got excited. The boys had called her "Squeaky Mouse" Peterson since she was in the third grade. They also joked that when she sat down, her ears popped.

The I.O. of O.G. members were blissfully unaware of such comments, and they met every two weeks to listen to "Select Readings from the Masters" and other literary offerings by the members. At their second gathering, Emma had presented "Ten Hard Words: Correct Pronunciation and Spelling."

She also became a member of the Women's Relief Corps and the purely social Alto Idem Club. And she had sent away for and received a medal recognizing her as the daughter of a Civil War veteran.

All of these goings-on, of course, had been in addition to her church activities under the leadership of the Reverend Doctor Bushnell. She continued her membership in the Epworth League, whose motto was spelled out in the tiny letters arranged in a circle around the little pin on her bosom. It said "LOOK UP—LIFT UP," if you could squint and screw your head around enough to make it out.

This was the young adult group of the church that met on Sunday nights. There was a prayer, a scripture reading, and a talk by one of the members, followed by "refreshments." On one occasion, Emma's topic of presentation had been "How Can Our League Make Our Town Better?"

Meanwhile, she had kept an eye out for a suitable suitor. And as is often the case, she had found one in a seemingly unlikely place: her own hometown.

He was Albert (Bert) Dockendorf, one of the twin sons of an early pioneer family who owned a 650-acre farm seven miles from

Cousin Emma and the Great Bicycle Rebellion

Highmore. The German lad was a handsome blond with a calm demeanor and a strong constitution. He boasted the mustache of the day, and his blue eyes were open and frank. And he was some five years older than Emma.

The two rediscovered one another on a sleigh ride for the young adults of the community, organized by the Alto Idem Club, and a courtship began. It continued for more than a year, and it was a carefully supervised affair in which the couple was rarely alone. There were church socials, there recitals, the Chatauqua, and songfests at their parents' homes. And there was an occasional buggy ride for two on moonlit nights in crisp autumn weather.

But any kind of intimacy was difficult, because America and small-town Iowa, like England before it, had come down with a galloping case of Victorian prudery. It was particularly noticeable in women's clothes.

Over their whale-bone corsets, which were nearly impenetrable, the female of the day was weighted down with voluminous layers of petticoats and finally a skirt that reached almost to the floor. Therefore, the most erotic part of the female body (according to many a young swain) was the ankle.

The word "leg" was never used, and even "limb" brought a gasp from well-bred ladies. The legs of grand pianos in many a home were discreetly draped in shawls, lest they foster lustful thoughts in the young men who came calling. So even before a young girl struggled into her first corset, she was instilled with the sanctity of self-restraint.

Molding young girls like Emma into paragons of virtue, however, had not been easy, according to the remembrances of Iowa professor Winifred Van Etten. Rules that were a combination of Victorian gentility and church morality were imposed by imperious mothers.

Emma and her friends never parted their hair on the side; boys did that. And everybody knew about the bad end to which whistling girls came.

A lady was told not to look in the doors of the blacksmith shop as she went by nor walk on any street where there was a livery or a saloon. Also, any dancing that involved touching was frowned upon—even the waltz.

In such a social climate, it was a wonder there was not a period of zero population growth. But Emma and her Bert had persevered in

The Potluck Dinner that Went Astray

their courtship, adhering to the rules of society as they understood them.

They had been married on a snowy February fourth in 1890 by the Reverend Doctor Bushnell. And they had set up housekeeping on a small farm about a mile from Highmore.

As a modern couple, Emma and Bert sought the civilization afforded by access to the advantages of the nearby town, and Bert became a sort of a gentleman farmer. They had some chickens and cows and two farm dogs, whose main activity seemed to consist of panting in the summer heat from a perch on the back stoop.

Both Emma and Bert had a lot of time on their hands, and she filled it by joining some additional organizations. She became a member of the oxymoronically named Royal Neighbors, a self-help secular group. As a young matron, she became more active in her church work as a member of the Ladies Aid Society and the Women's Foreign Missionary Society, but she did drop out of the Epworth League. It was now too young for her.

The birth of her daughter, Hazel, in 1892 had demanded her attention and occupied her time for awhile. The birth of her son, Clifford, the next year increased her mothering duties. but as the children grew up and went off to school, she became a bit bored.

And as the *fin de siecle,* with all its promises, came and went, Emma really became restive. She was weary of much of the sameness in life, and she chafed at the restrictions placed on her and other women. The countless meetings and gatherings seemed routine, and with the demise of the I.O. of O.G. (because most of the members were now also preoccupied with their own marriages and children), she found little intellectual stimulation.

But in that exciting year of 1900, the population of Highmore reached 4,267. The town was becoming a regional shopping center. Although the streets were still only dirt, the sidewalks downtown were paved. The town also boasted of six saloons to serve thirsty patrons. The village was beginning to live up to its name.

Some residents had telephones, and a few automobiles began to appear on the streets. And Emma began to notice another new contraption that was becoming popular in small-town America: the bicycle.

Although a machine to carry one forward had been invented early in the 1800s, such "velocipedes" were primitive affairs that required

Cousin Emma and the Great Bicycle Rebellion

the riders to propel them by moving their feet along the ground in a straight line. But around 1834, a Scotsman had invented a machine that could be steered and, more important, put in motion with pedals.

From there it was but a small step to the bikes that had a big, high wheel in front and a little wheel in back. They were called "ordinaries" in America and "penny farthings" in England. Of course, no lady could operate one, for her voluminous skirts made the mounting of the contraption difficult and the operation of it impossible.

But the big bikes evolved into the smaller "safety" bikes. They had same-size wheels, similar to those of today. They featured chain drives and braking systems. There was even a tandem bike, which allowed two people to ride on it.

That innovation had been romanticized by a popular song. But the idea of Daisy sitting sidesaddle on the back seat while being propelled by her beau scandalized many! Such freedom was shameful! A lady could even use one foot to pedal if she wanted to!

The final straw came when the manufacturers came up with a woman's bike in which the connecting bar between the front wheel and the seat was dropped down to accommodate a lady's skirts. She could straddle the seat! This was calumny!

Preachers rushed to condemn the new variation, and the Reverend Doctor Bushnell of Highmore, Iowa, was not far behind. In a scathing sermon on an otherwise beautiful Sabbath morn, he told his members that the device undermined feminine modesty, charm, and even morality!

A woman risked destroying her reputation if she climbed aboard one of those conveyances, he thundered. And if she donned one of the new-fangled trouser-skirts in order to provide her with even more freedom as she sat astride the vehicle—well!—she was surely headed straight for hell!

And besides, he said, according to many physicians, bicycling could damage a woman's private areas and lead to infertility!

The congregation was taken aback. Never had they heard such a mighty blast fired at such a tiny target!

Emma sat listening in quiet bemusement. She had never thought of the bicycle in that way. It was fascinating! The preacher had made it sound so exciting, and while she didn't believe half of what he said about the physical dangers of bicycling (after all, he was a man), he surely did make it sound attractive!

The Potluck Dinner that Went Astray

So more out of curiosity than anything else, she walked into town the next morning to investigate the matter. She had her choice of bike shops, for there were two new ones in the village, but some perverse notion sent her into the establishment of "Midge the Midget."

His real name was Arno P. Bartle, but the only people who knew that were the folks at the bank he patronized on an occasional basis. Midge had washed up in town by chance—and he was a drinker. He had been left behind by the circus two years before after he got smashed and was in a fight and thrown in jail. As he figured it, he was bound to get drunk again and maybe eaten by a lion, and he was sick of traveling and being gaped at as the "Little Wild Man from Borneo." So he decided to hunker down in Highmore.

The tiny fellow was witty, full of aphorisms and similes, and he had a talent—when he was sober, that is. He was quite simply a three-foot crackerjack salesman!

When he got to going, the guys said, he could pee on your boots and convince you that it was raining. The ladies maintained that on a good day he could talk a hen into plucking herself—when he was sober, that is.

But Midge was seldom in that condition. For his first few months in town, he had merely tried to stay one day ahead of yesterday. He had terrible anger at the fates that had spawned him and a mighty desire to relieve it.

So he visited the town's six saloons until he found one to his liking. And he began to spend a lot of time there. When his banker and doctor remonstrated with him about his overindulgence, he complained to his new drinking buddies with the words of that old Scottish lament: "They talk of my drinking but never of my thirst."

And, Midge added, he was still a work in progress. His avowed intention was to become the tallest midget in the world. "The Lord isn't done with me yet," he cackled.

He was fond of such quotations. On the lonely nights when he was not drinking, he retired to his rooms at the Hotel Martin and the company of his collection of books. He was particularly fond of Charles Dickens and identified strongly with *David Copperfield* and his unhappy childhood, but he found the much-loved *Christmas Carol* a bit sentimental for his taste.

Midge felt a kinship with the author and many of his characters in their love of spirits. Dickens, his friends, and the people who occupied

Cousin Emma and the Great Bicycle Rebellion

his books were prodigious consumers of booze. As a character in *Barnaby Rudge* rhapsodied, "It brightens the eye, improves the voice, [and] imparts a new vivacity to one's thoughts and conversation."

Suiting his actions to those words, Midge was prone to climb upon the bar on particularly salubrious evenings and regale his drinking comrades with other quotes from Dickens. Striking a stentorian pose, the little guy would stretch himself to his fullest height, lower his voice an octave, and with upraised arm and finger proclaim:

In the proverbs of Solomon, you will find the following words: "May we never want a friend in need, nor a bottle to give him."

His orations were usually much longer, but they were so entertaining that the bartenders often gave him drinks on the house, and on many an evening—in Dickens' words—"Down poured the wine like oil on a blazing fire." The night usually ended when the little fellow's legs gave way under him.

The binges, however, presented Midge with hangovers so bad that on some mornings he drank enough water to float the Rock of Ages. When his drinking comrades teased him about his perpetual red eyes, he often groaned, "You should see 'em from my side!"

His first business venture in town had been as a sales representative for a firm that made pictures of Jesus with eyes that follow you. He sold them to the Christian owners of the hotels and rooming houses in Highmore and the surrounding area for placement in the rooms. The intent was to discourage any sexual goings-on by the guests.

For the truly gullible, he had autographed pictures of Moses for sale, which went over big at revival meetings.

While Midge was extremely successful in these endeavors, he kept having to expand his territory in order to gain new customers. And traveling to strange towns increased his innate fear of big dogs and gave him the shakes, for he said he felt as vulnerable as a wooden Indian in a forest fire. The hounds in Highmore knew him and never bothered him, so he took his profits from the Jesus and Moses picture sales and invested them in the bike shop.

He was there on that bright Monday morning when Emma dropped in. And he was sober, for the saloons had all been closed on the preceding day in honor of the Sabbath. Before the hour was done, he had sold her a bike and given her a riding lesson.

The Potluck Dinner that Went Astray

Midge also developed a lot of respect for Emma during that encounter. He recognized the courage it took to defy her minister, for word had spread rapidly about the previous day's sermon. So when she left the shop and began wheeling her new purchase home, she went with his admiration and goodwill.

Bert was working on the side of the barn when Emma arrived. He was so astonished at the sight of her and her contraption that he dropped his hammer on one of the dogs. One look at her beaming countenance silenced any anti-bike remarks he might have made, however, and before long he was helping her learn to ride the thing in their backyard.

Well sir, the news that staid-and-steady Emma had bought a bike went through town like a prairie fire. Led by Squeaky Mouse and Famy B., women from the Alpha Idem and the Women's Relief Corps descended on Midge, demanding bikes. Even some of the members of the Ladies Home Missionary Society of her church went to Midge, seeking the device. A sort of dam had been broken, and before long he had back orders for the thing.

And as they became more proficient at the handling of the contraption, the ladies began riding in groups and making excursions into the countryside. The fresh air was invigorating and the exercise redeeming, for it was often followed by restorative tea or lemonade, little sandwiches, and conversation on the porch of one of the riders.

At the parsonage, the Reverend Doctor Bushnell scowled and yelled at his wife. His humor was not improved by the sound of the bells on the handlebars of the bikes of some of the riders, who teasingly jingled them as they passed by his door. Some people began calling the whole thing "The Great Bicycle Rebellion."

And in a sense it was, a tentative first step in the long march toward the liberation of the female population of the town. As the perpetrator of the action, Emma began to bask in the admiration of her colleagues and friends. But her Christian conscience bothered her.

So she set out to square accounts with Christ's messenger here on earth, and one cloudy Tuesday morning she visited upon the Reverend Doctor Bushnell. He was in his study overlooking the street and saw her coming up the walk, so he had a brief moment to prepare for her unscheduled visit.

But he was his usual uninspired self and could do little else but re-explain his unchanging position about the evils of bicycle riding for

Cousin Emma and the Great Bicycle Rebellion

the female sex. And he asked her as a Christian lady (and relative) to repent and give it up.

Cousin Emma would have none of it. Her jaw turned to cement, and a sort of simmering heat took over her heart as she left the study.

And when the budding women's suffrage movement sought her out to assist them in its endeavors to gain the vote, she was flattered and decided to join up. Its cause was a lot more important than that of any other group she belonged to and a lot more significant than bike riding.

The Iowa Women's Suffrage Association had been in existence since the mid-1800s, but it had made only a few faltering steps toward any real impact in the face of much ridicule by the men folk. The branch in Highmore had just been plodding along, content to hold some ill-attended meetings. After a long, two-year gestation, the group had recently issued a six-point plan for the local chapter. (It was supposed to have been a ten-pointer, but they had sort of lost interest along the way.)

One of the points, however, was a pledge to increase the visibility and promotional efforts of the organization. Emma and her bicycle cohorts fit neatly into that objective. For her part, with alacrity Emma took on a leadership role in the group. She liked being the center of attention and discovered that she had a talent for management and inspiration. And the goals of the group were most compatible with her emerging independence.

The Iowa constitution originally confined voting rights to "white male citizens," but after the Civil War an amendment took out the word "white" and thereby extended the vote to black men. And in 1894 Iowa women had been given the right to vote in municipal bond and school board elections. Now, in the new century, they were seeking full voting rights.

But the women needed the men in order to change the situation. To amend the U.S. Constitution to give women the vote throughout the country meant getting their support. And so the women had to enlist their husbands to the cause, as well as hundreds—and even millions—of other persons of the masculine persuasion.

When he wasn't laughing at the absurdity of a woman voting, however, the typical Highmore male began any argument, in what was beginning to be called "The Great Debate," with the Victorian

The Potluck Dinner that Went Astray

conviction that a woman's place was in the home. His vote represented the family interest in the political world, for "father knew best."

Besides, women were morally superior to men. They had higher ideals and were refined. An association with dirty politics and cigar smoke would debase them.

But this special morality also became a rallying point for those who were in favor of women's suffrage. Because they were so morally superior, some argued, women were obliged to develop a greater influence over men. By voting, they could do so.

So the two sides agreed on one thing anyway: woman's unique place in the overall scheme of things. The anti-feminists claimed that women should not have the vote because they were special. For the very same reason, the suffragettes said they should have the vote.

The Reverend Doctor Bushnell took notice of Cousin Emma's increased activity in the suffrage movement, particularly when she began to attract some of the ladies of his church into the troup. So he finally devoted a sermon one Sunday morning to the subject.

He was, not surprisingly, opposed to women's suffrage, and he found some scripture in 2 Peter (where men are exhorted to make their elections sure) to back him up. So he railed against those who supported the movement, calling them Philistines who threatened the home and family life of all Christian people. Most members also knew that he couldn't have taken any other posture if he wanted to maintain the goodwill of the men in his congregation. Besides, support of the notion would have meant change.

After the sermon, Emma's Christian conscience acted up again, and on the next afternoon—again uninvited—she visited the pastor in his study. He once again saw her coming up the walk, and, though he was thus forewarned, as usual he was uninspired and simply launched again into a scriptural defense of his position against women voting.

But of course, his rhetoric only served to fan Emma's ardor for the cause and strengthen her resolve. She flounced out and plunged into her suffragette work with even more vigor.

Emma discovered and adopted as the chapter's motto the slogan of *The Revolution,* a national women's rights publication founded by Elizabeth Cady Stanton and Susan B. Anthony. It trumpeted "MEN—Their Rights and Nothing More. WOMEN—Their Rights and Nothing Less." Posters and handouts bearing the slogan began to appear around town.

Cousin Emma and the Great Bicycle Rebellion

She even inspired her old-fashioned German mother-in-law to compose a tract titled "Women's Rights—and Men's Wrongs," which she handed out on street corners. Seeing Emma's passion and sensing the increasing momentum of the movement, her husband Bert kept his silent counsel and therefore his otherwise domestic tranquility.

Emma's biggest accomplishment that year was the organization of a parade in support of the cause. Some sixty ladies (all dressed in white with purple sashes across their chests spelling out the chapter's slogan) marched down the dusty main street of Highmore. They carried banners and posters with rallying mottos painted on them. The aggregation was followed by a pickup brass band of seven feminists playing martial airs and liberation tunes.

The parade made quite a stir and attracted a number of spectators, for Emma had wisely scheduled it for a Saturday evening, just before the closing time of the stores along the way. The sidewalks were packed with farmers and their families who had come to town for their weekly shopping.

When he heard the commotion in his study at the parsonage at the end of Main Street, the Reverend Doctor Bushnell scowled and yelled at his wife. His humor didn't improve when he perceived that the band music and rallying cries increased in intensity as they approached his house.

The music and noise also attracted Midge, who had been assuaging his thirst at his favorite tavern on the main drag since noon. He became incensed!

He was, after all, an A-mer-i-can citizen, a male, and a voter. Perhaps because of his small stature, he took those responsibilities more seriously than most, even though he was often so loaded on election days that he couldn't see the side of the voting booth he was in.

He admired Emma, but this was different. So, spurred by masculine indignation and drunken righteousness, he raced to his shop and got out the small bike he had made to promote his business. And as the parade reached the parson's house and turned around to march back up the street again, Midge joined in.

Shouting obscenities and "NEVER! NEVER!" he circled the marching women on his little bike, weaving tipsily and waving and hallooing. He rode in and out and around and about the marchers in a drunken haze, and in his efforts to disrupt the proceedings, he tried to

The Potluck Dinner that Went Astray

wobbly steer the contraption between the rows. But the ladies simply closed ranks, and Midge veered woozily off.

He did somehow manage to bounce the tiny bike up on the sidewalk, however, scattering spectators and knocking over the displays of clothes and vegetables put out by the merchants in front of their stores. And as he careened out of control down the sidewalk and through the crowd, his eyes became unfocused, and he seemed ready to pass out as he clung desperately to the side of the little speeding vehicle.

But just before Midge scraped the ground, he shook his head, pulled himself up, and somehow steered it back onto the street. Righting himself further, he zigzagged crazily down to the end of the block. There, in an effort to gain suicidal momentum and an angle of attack, he paused for a moment, gathering strength. Then, pedaling furiously with his little legs a blur, he raced full tilt at Emma, whom he deemed to be the symbol of this heresy and who was conveniently marching in the very front rank of the suffragettes!

Midge's front wheel hit a rock imbedded in the street at about the same time that his final scream of "N-E-V-E-R!" reached its climax. The bike stopped, but Midge kept going!

For years afterward, folks said he reminded them of the human cannonball in his old circus. Midge traveled about twenty feet through the air in a trajectory that landed him almost directly in front of Emma.

Some who were there insisted later that he had flown at least forty feet. Others said that he emitted a sort of terrified whooshing sound as he flew in an arc through the air, and that he made an awful thump when he hit the ground at Emma's feet.

At any rate, there Midge lay, unconscious in a lump in the middle of the street. The marchers straggled to a halt, and the band gradually tootled down into silence. Emma knelt down and picked the little body up. Motioning to Bert, who was standing on the sidewalk nearby, she carried the inert form to their new Model T, which was parked over on Elm Street.

They took him home and called the doctor. Midge had regained consciousness by that time, but he was delirious. Doc Joynt said he had a severe concussion, a broken shoulder blade and wrist, and some terribly bad bruises and cuts all up and down his right side. He was probably saved from further injury by the amount of alcohol in his

Cousin Emma and the Great Bicycle Rebellion

body, which had made him relaxed when he hit the ground, said Doc. And he shouldn't be moved too much, Doc warned.

So Emma became a nursemaid to the little fellow. She and Bert moved a bed into the library room off the parlor. She fed and washed Midge, and he gradually gained strength and a measure of coherence, although he was still very hazy about what had happened. And as the days went by, he and Emma talked a lot and developed a real friendship.

At about this time, she was approached by the leaders of the Women's Christian Temperance Union (WCTU) who had taken notice of her leadership in the bicycle rebellion and the suffrage movement. Could she help them, they wondered.

The WCTU had been trudging along with limited success, for the America of the day still clung to the heavy drinking habits of its pioneers. The organization had been founded in the 1870s, but its name was really a misnomer. Prohibition, not temperance, was its aim.

The group's purpose was to put an end to drinking and prostitution and—while they were at it—smoking as well. Under the leadership of Frances Willard, and with Carrie Nation and her axe-breaking bottles and kegs in saloons, the organization had set about the task of changing the entire moral climate of the United States.

The group's biggest argument against "demon rum" was that it often acted as a sort of male aphrodisiac, which—to many women of the time who looked at sex as at best a submission and at worst a degradation—was not to be tolerated. Besides, drink led to abandoned families and starving women and children.

Few reasonable people of the time would have denied that the country's out-of-control drinking habits would benefit from some sort of reform. Temperance? Yes. Prohibition? No!

And so the the battle had been joined between the wets and the dries. Because the temperance ladies knew the only way they were going to reach their objective was to obtain the vote, the WCTU had aligned itself in many communities with the suffragettes. Now it sought to do so in Highmore.

The dries tended to favor giving women the vote because they thought women would vote against booze and other vices. Those who liked having a beer now and then were against giving women the vote because they feared their suds would be taken away from them.

The Potluck Dinner that Went Astray

So when Cousin Emma decided to join up with the WCTU in common cause, many would-be suffragette supporters walked away. Men who had no particular objection to women's suffrage had the strongest possible objection to the elimination of one of life's little pleasures.

This included Bert, for, though he was modest in his drinking habits, he viewed the WCTU position with a shudder. When his friends asked him if he couldn't do something about his wife, he just rolled his eyes and murmured, "I try; God knows I try."

But Midge, who by now had straightened his brains out and become a sort of unofficial advisor-confidant of Emma's, counseled that even though he didn't agree with her, "if one was to get an egg, she shouldn't worry whether the chicken likes her or not." And so Emma soldiered on.

She began to have meetings and planning sessions for the WCTU in the parlor next to the library room where Midge was recovering. The ladies decided to set up a temperance booth at the fall fair and establish patrols in front of the taverns on Saturday nights in order to cajole those entering or leaving to sign "the pledge." And they developed a new petition for circulation and rehearsed and adopted as their official anthem a stirring march by Charles M. Fillmore titled "The Saloon Must Go." The song had four verses, but the chorus said it all:

> *We stand for Pro-hi-bi-tion,*
> *The utter de-mo-li-tion*
> *Of all this curse of mis-er-y and woe,*
> *Complete ex-ter-mi-na-tion,*
> *Entire an-ni-hi-la-tion*
> *The saloon must go!*

It was a rouser! And it evidently reached down deep and touched something from Midge's Baptist childhood in Claxton, Georgia, the fruitcake capital of the world. Before long, he was joining in on the chorus from the adjoining room. And after the second meeting and rehearsal of the song, the little guy announced that he was ready to sign the pledge!

Midge's trip through the air had, in effect, sobered him up and altered his mind permanently, he said. Furthermore, he would advise and help the crusaders in luring men away from the bottle! He confessed to them all that he had often been so drunk that if he had been

Cousin Emma and the Great Bicycle Rebellion

shot in the head, he would have had to sober up to die. And as a drinker of Olympic proportions, he was, he sobbed, well-qualified to teach the group about the evils of booze and how to combat it!

Midge's conversion was so startling that it threatened to blow the ladies' skirts right up over their heads! Famy B. fainted dead away and had to be revived with fans and smelling salts!

But as they all gathered around his sickbed, Midge took the pledge, and Emma pinned the ribbon to the lapel of his robe, signifying his new status. They all sang the anthem again, and then Midge set about educating the women in the ways of drinking men.

First of all, he said, they had to understand why men liked to wrap their lips around a glass. It was partly the comradery. A sort of wacky bonding occurred, although he assured them it wasn't as strong as when women shopped together.

Some men drank to forget their problems and some to forget a lost love. And some tippled (he said apologetically) because they maintained that their wife was so ugly that she only looked good through the bottom of an empty glass.

Some guys were, of course, down on their luck and so broke they couldn't hardly pay attention. Many, he said, drank just to feel good for a change. And he passed on some tavern wisdom that said one should never argue with a drunk, a skunk, or a woman.

That last bit was most important, he said. It was useless to stand around outside the saloons pushing pledges at the boys and trying to argue with them. Besides, it was dangerous. One saloon was so bad that it had a sign on the front door that proclaimed: "GOOD BOOZE AND BAD COMPANY!" Another one was so awful that they charged you a dollar to get in and two to get out.

If they were going in, the guys had a monumental desire for liquid refreshment. If they were coming out, they were usually wobbly-butt, knee-walkin', toilet-hangin' drunk. And whether they were coming or going, the fellows had other things on their minds at that time and about as much use for an argument as Noah had for a foghorn on the ark.

No sir, it was better to hit them when they were most vulnerable: on the morning after, with a crushing hangover, when they were swearing they would never touch another drop, when their throats were dry and their heads were in their hands. *Carpe diem!*

The Potluck Dinner that Went Astray

Get 'em when they felt so bad in the bright morning light that if the day were a fish, they'd throw it back!

So the ladies made up bunches of flowers, with Bible texts and the pledge attached, for distribution to those who emerged from the town jail after sleeping off a Saturday night toot. As the boys staggered out, the ladies swooped in. And it worked!

They picked up five converts in the first three weeks of effort, and so they made the Sunday Morning Rendezvous (as they began to call it) a regular part of their operation. By this time, Midge had fully recovered and left Emma's care and returned to his rooms at the hotel.

But he continued to help her, the WCTU, and the women's suffrage group over the next few years. One of his projects was to coach Emma and the other designated spokesperson for the two organizations in their speeches. For after listening to Emma one night at a Grange Hall rally, Midge gently told her that her oration was about as effective as a pint of whiskey split five ways.

He gave the speakers jokes and aphorisms and helped them with their diction. He reminded them that they were not talking to the people in the "amen corner." They needed to add a felicitous blend of whimsy and verve to their stilted rhetoric and starched demeanor, he said. He had some success.

Emma began to show occasional flashes of zip and by-golly jingo in her delivery. But the other lady was simply too serious about her cause and incapable of even a modest amount of sparkle, so Midge backed off.

But he taught them how to handle the inevitable hecklers with comeback lines. He told the ladies that if it got too bad to just go about their business and act as if the guy's mother didn't have any children that lived.

Over the years when the ladies became discouraged, Midge backed them up by observing that a toothpick started out as a log. And he inspired them by quoting from his favorite author—this time with an opposite effect. According to Midge, in *Sketches by Boz,* Dickens noted that

> If Temperance Societies would suggest an antidote against hunger, filth, and foul air . . . gin palaces would be numbered among the things that were.

Cousin Emma and the Great Bicycle Rebellion

Midge pointed out that, although the progress had been slow over the past few years on both the temperance and women's suffrage fronts, they were at least beginning to hoe in the short rows. It was now 1914, and eleven states had given women the right to vote, while seven western states were contemplating or had passed prohibition laws.

Progress was reaching home. Bert had come around and now at least discussed the issues with Emma in a calm and reasonable manner. So her familial and Christian conscience was clear, and she sought no audience with her minister.

But down at the parsonage, the Reverend Doctor Bushnell was mired in a dilemma. He had no problem with the WCTU and Cousin Emma's involvement with it. The Methodists were teetotalers by official decree, and he had supported the local chapter—albeit somewhat coolly—because he knew some of the male members in his congregation indulged in a snort at times. And for that matter, rumor had it that the head of the Ladies Aid Society was known to take a nip or two from the cooking sherry on occasion.

But the Reverend still had a problem with the women's suffrage issue and any change in the status quo. While many of the men in his congregation had begun to come around to at least halfheartedly support the right of women to vote, he was hesitant.

One night, though, his usually quiet and long-suffering wife, who had become a silent supporter of "the cause" and an admirer of Cousin Emma, got him to sit down for a chat about the matter. A fairly fierce light was in her eyes, and her arguments were intense.

Her points were so well-taken that he rose with the promise to at least be quiet about women's suffrage from there on in. And the next day he invited his annoying cousin Emma over for afternoon tea.

It was the first time he had invited her to visit him in his study, and it was a kind-of-truce affair. The good parson was as usual uninspired, but he did manage to repeat many of his wife's points of the night before. And while Emma had hoped for an endorsement of the suffrage movement, she was pleased to at least receive his promise of silence on the matter. The battle had been sort-of won.

And so Emma returned home to resume her work. She was by now an accomplished leader and speaker and very much in demand. But as the years had moved on, she had become a bit bored with the

The Potluck Dinner that Went Astray

topics of bicycling, temperance, and suffrage. And so she began to search for something new and interesting to apply her talents to, for, as she had discovered, causes are addictive.

She thought she had found a new cause in vegetarianism, but Midge pointed out that there was little chance of her prevailing in that matter, for she lived in the top pork-producing state in the nation. So she cast about for another calling to satisfy her social-action needs and Christian belief—"Not my will, but Thine be done." And she finally found one!

One bright fall morning, Cousin Emma got out her bike and pedaled rapidly toward the parsonage in a buzz of excitement! She was on a new mission! And since her minister had been so accommodating lately, this time she'd get his approval in advance!

The Reverend Doctor Bushnell was in his own ecstasy of contemplation, working on next Sunday's sermon, which he had tentatively titled "God: Bass or Baritone?" He was knee-deep in pondering what significance there was in the fact that *dog* spelled backwards was *God*.

So when he saw from the window in his study Cousin Emma wheeling her bike up the walk, he could only groan wearily: "Oh Lord, what now?"

What new cause was she into? How could he handle it? What could he say or do?

And then it came to him!

He threw up his hands in ecstacy and said, "I'll leave her and her progressive ideas for someone else to deal with!" Inspired by this thought, he slipped quickly out the back door and down the alley and went for a long walk.

When he got home that afternoon, the good Reverend Doctor Bushnell sent off his retirement notice to his ecclesiastical superior in Sioux City. And the next day he went out and bought two bicycles—for himself and his wife—from Midge the Midget.

* * *

In 1915, the Iowa state legislature passed a law requiring statewide prohibition. In 1916, however, Iowa voters defeated a proposal that would have given women the vote in that state.

The constitutional amendment requiring national prohibition was ratified by the required number of states in 1919. It was repealed, however, in 1933.

Cousin Emma and the Great Bicycle Rebellion

But on August 20, 1920, the Nineteenth Amendment to the Constitution of the United States was ratified, giving women the vote throughout the nation. It has not been repealed.

And bicycling—by both men and women—is today the country's third largest recreational activity, with 54.3 million people participating in it, more than 50 percent of whom are women.

Funny, He Doesn't Look Presbyterian

The congregation had a problem. The minister was old and worn out. He had been the shepherd of the people for nearly thirty-five years and had grown with the small church that was snuggled comfortably in the suburb of an eastern city. He had come to them as a young go-getter with a New England accent that was more Presbyterian than he was. And he was, in fact, responsible for much of the growth of the church—both in membership and in mission.

But progress had stopped almost ten years ago, and while the membership hadn't actually declined, the church was atrophying. Community outreach had all but dried up.

In the last few years, the pastor had seemed to adhere to a policy that nothing should ever be done for the first time. He was all for progress, the parson said, as long as it didn't change anything.

He had been a short fellow to begin with, and as the years rolled on, he had seemed to shrink even more—perhaps from the weight of the office. He owned a small paunch now and walked with an odd sort of gait that suggested his shoes maybe had become too tight.

The parson was much beloved. He had the patience to deal with church members who were somewhere in their own land—an ability to listen to those whose fan was missing one blade. While most persons of the congregation looked at one another in dismay at their fellow members' lapses in logic, he simply nodded encouragingly. He had built his reputation on his kind and compassionate nature.

But now he was seen by most folk as a sort of lovable, durable relic. His older ministerial colleagues in the regional governing body—the presbytery—affectionately called him by his last name, Toplady, while the younger ones always prefaced his name with the honorific "Old" for the same reason. And he was slipping.

On some Sunday mornings he would approach the pulpit and ceremoniously open the Big Book to the place where he had put the elegant marker to indicate the spot to begin the Scripture reading. But often as not, a look of utmost consternation would cross his face. He would slowly flip first right and then left through the pages.

Funny, He Doesn't Look Presbyterian

Sometimes minutes would pass before he found the right page or surrendered the search after discovering that he had marked the spot correctly after all. And shaking his head at the demons who had once again got together to foul up the worship service, he would begin to read.

His preaching also became erratic, and he would ramble on sometimes during his sermons. At other times, he would lose his train of thought and fall silent while looking quizzically up at the ceiling for a moment or two, as if seeking divine inspiration.

And at the benediction, he started to habitually include a prayer for the "little people of this world." He finally confessed to one of the worship committee members that he was talking about all those—like himself—who were under 5'5".

In other church activities, he also began to act strangely. One day while discussing philosophy, he confounded an elder by agreeing with Heideggen's belief that no one else could die for you. But he maintained that a more important existentialist—Delmore Schwartz—had summed up life better in his statement that no one else could take a bath for you.

In a Bible study class, he spent thirty minutes discussing the fact that some scholars maintained that Adam and Eve ate a pomegranate rather than an apple.

He also advanced the idea that Jesus may have had a wife. It was just possible, he offered, that Mary Magdalene was not just the prostitute that orthodox interpretation makes her out to be. Some folk in Alabama think that she was also the "lost bride of Christ."

And he said there was also some debate about the Lord's death and resurrection. Some people believe Jesus lived to a ripe old age in India and point to a grave there to buttress their theory.

Old Toplady became fascinated with children's hand puzzles. He'd spend all afternoon in his study some days, just trying to get the two little BB's into the eyes of the tiger.

And on some mornings, he startled the church secretary with renditions of a song he had begun to believe he had written about a miner and his daughter Clementine who had become lost. He strapped on a bass drum from the nursery school and, singing lustily, tooled around the office like the bunny in the Duracel commercials. And he whispered to her that he had a feeling he was being followed by Bolivians.

The Potluck Dinner that Went Astray

The final straw came when he asked for a special meeting of the local church ruling-body, the Session, to discuss the implications of his discovery of the secret meaning of the initials of the P.E.O. organization. He said that P.E.O. stood for Presbyterians Eat Onions, and he demanded to know what the Session was going to do about stopping this blasphemy.

In the best traditions of the British constabulary, two of the elders gently took him home. "Come along now, sir. All proper and orderly, sir. Just this way, sir." To his protests, they patiently assured him: "You'll be heard, sir. All in good time, sir, all in good time."

But of course, he never was. His long-suffering wife finally persuaded him to retire. She had been married to a clergyman for more than fifty years, and as she confided to her sister, "To be married to one that long requires a good deal of imagination."

So she sent off for a booklet entitled "How to Start an Ostrich Ranch," published by the United States Ostrich Association of Amarillo, Texas. She did so, she sighed, because the parson had lately expressed an interest in entering that field, after he read that the lanky eight-foot bird was destined to become the "low-fat meat of the 21st century."

The publication soon arrived and informed them that the flightless birds from Africa make good eating and a fine investment. Ostrich meat is lower in fat and calories than chicken, and ostriches propagate faster, eat less, and require fewer acres of land than cattle.

Moreover, the leathery skin, eyelashes, feathers, and even the toenails of the weird-looking creatures could be sold at a good profit. In short, said the Association, Americans will soon be carving ostrich legs instead of turkey at Thanksgiving. Get in this field now!

So Old Toplady retired, and he and his wife packed up their belongings and took off for Texas. No one ever heard much from—or of—them again.

The church formed an interim pastor search committee, which promptly set out on the task of finding a person who would temporarily fill the pulpit. And it found one in the Reverend Irene Hancock.

She was one of those perpetually floating sorts of people who claimed that her religious calling was to move around a lot in serving God. She had made her profession one of filling in for a year or so in a church before moving on when that church hired a permanent pastor.

Funny, He Doesn't Look Presbyterian

The Reverend Irene was proud of her handwriting and boasted of the hours she spent in her kitchen devising a recipe for the pumpkin pickles that people ate during colonial days. She was enamored of the vegetable, she said, because pickles were mentioned quite often in the Bible.

The new interim minister loved alliteration. She and her husband had three grown boys, all named after famous men. There was a Herbert Hoover Hancock, a Hubert Humphrey Hancock, and in what surely must have been a desperate reach, a Horace Heidt Hancock. This was a bow to a 1930s bandleader.

In the pulpit, she was less than inspired. Her rhetoric was so astonishing that you had to hear it not to believe it. And in her administration of church affairs, she was less than forceful. Although a Presbyterian is one who dares to be cautious, she took things to the extreme. Her most common directive was "Maybe—and that's final!"

Her growing number of critics in the congregation began to understand that her peripatetic ecclesiastical life was similar to an old vaudevillian's stage strategy. Both moved around a lot to create a moving target for the vegetables that might be tossed at them. Most of the members of the church began to look forward to the time of the Reverend Irene's departure.

And so it was with a sense of increasing urgency that the Permanent Pastoral Nominating Committee pursued its charge. Its members had been elected from the church membership after the interim pastor had been chosen. The group had been engaging in its activities in a sort of desultory way, feeling that as long as an interim pastor was on hand, they had all the time in the world to find a permanent replacement for Old Toplady.

But now with the murmurings about the Reverend Irene gaining momentum, they began to realize that they should approach their task in a more vigorous manner. The committee had been meeting weekly, as prescribed by the presbytery, but most of the time was spent socializing. The committee, however, was pretty representative of the congregation.

The chair was a young, self-made, self-satisfied businessman who was too sincere by half and terribly pious. He liked to garden. His specialty was string beans. The vice-chair was a fetching housewife who wore earrings so large that dogs could jump through them and hats as

The Potluck Dinner that Went Astray

big as umbrellas. She squealed or squeaked (it was hard to tell which) at everything and secretly dreamed of bittersweet lust. People said she spent most of her time, outside of her committee work, reading bodice-rippers.

There was a housepainter who had never read more than a menu in his life and who felt that women were biologically defective and incapable of logical thought. Furthermore, he was convinced that they must be subjugated, lest they overwhelm men with their insatiable sexual demands. To counter him, there was a feminist midwife who believed that every woman's body was a holy vessel. She was a sort-of chip-on-the-shoulder radical who viewed all men with suspicion. And she put mace in her purse when she came to teach her Sunday School class every week.

Another committee member was a timid school librarian who secretly attended Wrestlemania matches because his job didn't really fulfill all of his emotional needs. Except for those excursions, he was duller than any Presbyterian had a right to be. The group also included an over-educated matron with a deep alto voice who, as a graduate of one of the Seven Sisters, was fond of quoting Aristotle to the effect that marriage was simply a matter of household management.

She usually disagreed with the committee's swing vote, a housewife of indeterminate age with eyes like a deer caught in the headlights of a car. This lady seemed to vary between the beliefs of a knee-jerk liberal who speculated that only blacks had a corner on life's pleasures and a rock-bound conservative who was certain that it was so. Her shilly-shally comments on any subject were usually challenged—just on principle—by the insurance salesman on the committee who was (he admitted) "bordering on handsome." His business success was directly related to his visibility in the congregation.

Rounding out the group was Mrs. Marguerite Peterson, a rotund accountant. She was a nice lady who never did or said anything—just sat there with her big body overflowing a chair. She uttered not a word at meetings. She was, in fact, the most un-Presbyterian of the lot.

The group now began to meet on a more serious basis. Matters were usually discussed in a cultured murmur, but on occasion one or two voices were raised in response to a particularly inane remark by the housepainter or the feminist.

Surrounding the more leisurely early meetings had been a feeling that the committee would recommend a woman for the post of permanent pastor. It was never discussed openly, but phone calls between members and one-on-one conversations in the parking lot after meetings led most everyone to that inclination.

In this matter, the committee was reflecting the times and feelings of many members of the congregation. The women's liberation movement of years past had finally filtered down and entered the thought processes of even the most stalwart Presbyterian. Most members had finally become persuaded that at least no great and lasting harm would ensue and that the walls of the sanctuary would remain standing if their new shepherd were to be a woman.

This sentiment was also partially the result of the gender makeup of the committee, in which the women outnumbered the men five to four. The amiable librarian had empathized with such a strategy, as did the businessman chair, who didn't want a fight, and the insurance salesman, who wanted to be seen as modern and politically correct. Only the housepainter would have objected if it had ever come to a vote.

But this was all before the temporary tenure of the Reverend Irene. Her idiosyncrasies and general incompetence as the interim pastor reflected on any female candidate for the permanent pastor's job. The committee was forced to privately and informally concede among themselves that given the rising feeling about her, it would be impossible to successfully nominate a woman for the permanent post.

Of course, none of this was discussed openly at the more serious committee meetings now. The strict protocol recommended by the presbytery was followed to the letter. There would be no sexual or racial discrimination of any kind—negative or positive—in the selection and hiring of the new permanent minister.

But there was still a sort of "what if" half-hearted sentiment among the congregation and the committee for some real change in leadership. Perhaps this was the moment, for no one wanted to hire just a younger version of Old Toplady. They didn't need, said some, another traditional blond, blue-eyed, WASP (White-Anglo-Saxon-Presbyterian). Maybe this was *the* time for change.

So the committee privately and individually thought through the possibilities. It was discouraging.

This was a congregation that, in its suburban haven, had only seen a black on the back of a garbage truck and a Jew as a character in one

The Potluck Dinner that Went Astray

of Shakespeare's plays. The members' concept of a migrant worker was someone who commuted to the city. An Oriental was out because they all looked alike, and one couldn't tell whether they were Japanese, Chinese, or Korean. American Indians lived out west somewhere just past the Hudson River and were responsible for the death of General George Armstrong Custer. And a Latino would not work out because Latinoes all had big extended families to support, and the church couldn't afford the salary necessary to feed them all.

The housewife with the big hats floated the idea that maybe they should think about hiring a convicted criminal. After all, wasn't Jeb Stuart Macgruder, who had served 218 days in prison for his role in covering up the Watergate break-in, now a Presbyterian minister in Kentucky? Besides, such types had a real sort of personal magnetism, she argued breathlessly.

But that notion didn't even get past the housepainter, and so the committee resigned itself privately and individually to taking potluck. There would be no hidden agenda. The committee members would simply examine the dossiers of the candidates in a truly impartial manner with no predispositions. And whatever candidates emerged, emerged.

So after examining more than 125 dossiers over the period of a year, the committee reached a concensus on five possible candidates. All were men, and one was clearly superior on the basis of his written credentials. After two more meetings, the group narrowed the choices to three, with the superior candidate still leading the pack.

And as was the custom, the committee selected three of its members to take to the road to interview and hear each candidate preach on a Sunday as a "visiting minister" at a neutral site. The chair went, along with the feminist and the wide-eyed housewife who could never make up her mind.

The first two candidates to be heard were young fellows who had served their apprenticeships in similar suburban churches as associate pastors and were ready to move up the ecclesiastical ladder. They had both been in charge of youth groups, served on minor church committees, and had diligently learned their jobs and the intricacies of dealing with white, middle-class, suburban parishioners at the feet of experienced ministers. They were both blond, and (although one unaccountably had brown eyes) each had the requisite perky wife and two charming kids—the PI (Presbyterian-Issued) tow-headed boy and

Funny, He Doesn't Look Presbyterian

girl. One of them even had experience in fund-raising at a nonprofit organization. The other was a better preacher.

The three committee members saved the visit to hear the candidate who was clearly superior—on paper at least—for last. He was the feminist's odds-on favorite for the post, based on his resume and other submitted documents, but she and her fellow committee members were in for a surprise.

The guy was black. Not tan or mulatto or light-skinned, but an ebony black African-American.

The employment form he had filled out and submitted to the committee contained no obvious indication of his race. There certainly was no box to check off one's race, and there was no indication that he was black from the schools he had attended. His college was a middle-class, liberal arts institution in the middle of the United States. And his seminary was as American mainstream as was his accent when he talked to the chair on the telephone to set up the meeting with the committee. Besides, he had been born in Davenport, Iowa.

In retrospect, said the chair, the committee members were naive. They should have spotted it.

The Reverend Addison's resume indicated that he had been a member of some multicultural-sounding groups in college and had later chaired ecumenical church organizations that apparently dealt with minority concerns. He had spent a year in South Africa on a study leave and had written passionately about his experiences there. And he was, after all, the associate pastor of an inner-city church in Detroit. In his written statement he had submitted to the committee, he had described his ministry to that congregation, which was about 50 percent black.

But this was all hindsight. When the three committee members walked into a church in Akron, Ohio (the neutral site) on that Sunday morning to hear him preach—and saw him for the first time—they were flabbergasted!

They looked at one another in consternation. Was there some sort of mistake? Wrong church? Wrong day? But no, there he was; and as they watched him lead the worship service, they began to settle down.

The Reverend Addison was a trim thirty-six-year-old who conducted the service with a relaxed dignity. He came across as an engaging person with an expressive face and a gentlemanly

The Potluck Dinner that Went Astray

personality. And when he rose to preach, the committee members were finally comfortable enough to be most attentive.

The good pastor had chosen for his topic the most difficult one for any minister: death. It was a daring subject, for he knew his future was on the line that Sunday. No congregation (and certainly no pastoral nominating cmmittee) ever really wanted to hear about mortality and the Grim Reaper. The subject made everyone uncomfortable. And to be confronted with the subject on a sunny Sunday morning—well! But the Reverend Addison had ignored the recommended lectionary for the week and had struck off on his own in dangerous waters.

He used as his takeoff point the recent death, from AIDS-related pneumonia, of the black tennis star Arthur Ashe. It was, he said, a model for everyone in the art of "going gently into that good night."

The tennis legend had been a great admirer of the distinguished theologian Dr. Howard Thurman. The Reverend Addison used one of that scholar's poems as his theme for the sermon:

> *How good it is to center down*
> *To sit quietly and see one's self pass quietly by!*
> *The streets of our minds seethe with endless traffic;*
> *Our spirits resound with clashings, with noisy silences.*
> *While something deep within hungers and thirsts for*
> *The still moment and the resting lull.*

The Reverend Addison spoke of the need for one to allow time for sitting and watching "one's self pass quietly by." He talked of the need for continued reflection in this world in preparation for the next. He ended with another quote from Dr. Thurman to the effect that "death is an event in life. It is something that occurs *in* life rather than something that occurs *to* life."

At the end, there was an awesome stillness in the sanctuary. The message was a profound and emotional, yet reasoned, discourse. It challenged the mind with an appealing honesty that made each listener feel a little wiser. After the Reverend Addison closed with a brief prayer, there were finally some stirrings among the congregation, along with appreciative murmurs and here and there a muffled and respectful "Amen."

All in all, it was a virtuoso performance. The young minister had spoken with eloquence and in a composed baritone voice. His vocal

Funny, He Doesn't Look Presbyterian

dynamics were outstanding, and he had used gestures sparingly but meaningfully. The three members of the committee were bowled over!

They were equally impressed when they met him that afternoon. He was affable as he answered their questions with a warm sincerity, and he seemed to radiate from within a wonderful generosity of spirit.

The three members of the committee were therefore unanimous in their enthusiasm for the candidacy of the Reverend Addison. Even the wishy-washy housewife was eagerly positive. So, armed with a tape recording of his sermon, they returned to report their findings to their fellow committee members.

And after hearing the glowing recommendation of the three representatives, listening to the sermon on the tape, and double-checking his references again, the committee members voted unanimously to invite the Reverend Addison to visit their community and church and meet with all of them. That visit also turned out to be a success, but it did foretell a bit about a potential problem.

Word leaked out that the committee was considering a black man, and veiled questions were slyly raised by one or two parishioners. Fortunately, the questions were addressed to the chair, who had the wisdom to calmly respond that indeed yes, "it was funny, he doesn't look Presbyterian." And then he shut up, leaving the questioners to ponder his answer in an awkward silence.

But the inquiries did raise the further question as to whether the congregation as a whole was ready to call a black man to be its spiritual leader. Was this the time for such a radical change? After all, as the housepainter pointed out, there was that old joke that the first Jewish president would be an Episcopalian—the moral being that people can accept only so much change at once.

But even he came around, and in the end the committee's vote to recommend the Reverend Addison to the entire church membership to be the permanent minister was unanimous. There was some discussion, however, as to how to present him to the congregation.

Traditionally, the candidate preached a sermon on some Sunday morning, and his résumé was circulated. After the service, he was escorted to an adjoining room, while the church membership voted to reject or accept him. In most cases, it was an automatic "yes" vote, because most congregations respected the thorough and exhaustive search process.

The Potluck Dinner that Went Astray

But this was different. The committee kicked around the idea of having him preach from behind a screen on that Sunday. That technique had found favor in the audition methods of some symphony orchestras, because it eliminated any consideration of the individual's physical personality as it affected musical ability—and for that matter, any consideration of sex or race.

But in the end, the committee decided to simply do it the old-fashioned way. It was honest and clean, and besides, by now most of the congregation had heard that the candidate was black.

So the Sunday date was set, and in spite of suggestions by the committee that he preach the sermon on death that had so impressed them, the Reverend Addison chose another topic. As he told his wife, his mother had tried desperately not to raise foolish children, and he was not about to tempt Presbyterian predestination by again charging into dangerous territory. So he pulled out an old tried-and-true sermon about the redemptive power of prayer that he had polished over many years and used it.

It was quite well-received. There were exchanged glances and some nods of approval among some of the younger church members. But close observers among the committee sensed an undercurrent of restlessness and hesitation in the sanctuary.

So when the Reverend Addison was escorted out to the fellowship hall to await the verdict, the tension in the place became palpable. This was an important vote that would change the lives of many people, and the members of the church felt the weight of it.

After his name was formally entered into nomination by the chair of the committee, the floor was open for discussion. The initial comments were laudatory and came largely from the younger members.

But as the meeting progressed, little concerns began to be expressed—mostly by the older members. Wasn't the Reverend Addison a bit young for such a responsibility? Did he have any experience in counseling all kinds of people? As a midwesterner, would he be comfortable in the east? And, most tellingly, did he have a background and understanding of "our suburban culture"?

Race was, of course, never mentioned. But it was the unspoken consideration. The Reverend Addison's demeanor was exemplary of course. He didn't fit any of the stereotypical images of blacks, and his sermon that morning, if not inspiring, was reasonable and comfortable.

Funny, He Doesn't Look Presbyterian

His credentials were all in order. The pastoral nominating committee had sifted through more than 126 candidates and had unanimously approved him. Everyone wanted some change, but were they really ready for this?

As the discussion continued, Mrs. Wyonna Gordon, a widow in her seventies, began fidgeting and tapping her cane on the floor from her seat in the back row pew on the right. Finally she rose slowly to her feet.

There was an instant hush. Here was one of the oldest and most revered members of the church. Here was a lady whose life as a Christian was an example for them all. And here was a lady whose financial contributions had balanced the budget of the church on more than one occasion!

Mrs. Gordon had been a member of the congregation for more than forty years and had "seen 'em come and go," as she often put it. She and her late husband had served as deacons and elders more than once. And over the years they had welcomed dilettantes and drunks to the church membership, and often had been cheered by their presence and disappointed by their actions.

The strong-willed dowager was a descendant of a Priscilla MacInzie of Glasgow, Scotland, who had emigrated to this country in 1636. From a Boston base, the family members had spread out over the continent and had made their money in lumber and land, frequently aligning themselves with sturdy young bucks to keep the blood line strong. As the family joke went, they married beneath them, as all women do.

The women of the family were independent, blunt-spoken, and invariably Republican. And it was this heritage of self-reliance and conservative wealth that the lady brought with her as she rose to her feet that Sunday morning.

Mrs. Gordon was brief and to the point. She reminded the congregation of the need for change. She said that the church members should reflect the larger society outside of their little suburban enclave. She pointed out that the pastoral nominating committee had spent over a year in coming up with this candidate. She told the people they ought to watch the "Bill Cosby" show on television. She ended her little talk by quoting from Ecclesiastes to the effect that there is a time for all seasons under heaven, and this was one of them!

The Potluck Dinner that Went Astray

She put it to them and sat down. Someone called the question, the ballots were distributed, and the congregation voted.

Oh, it wasn't unanimous—more like 197 to 46—but it was a big majority and a clear enough indication of the feelings of the congregation. The Reverend Addison became the new minister.

Over pink punch and cookies at the welcoming reception after the meeting, people were further charmed by his gentle graciousness. They were equally taken with his wife.

She enchanted them all by admitting that she lacked the usual attribute of a minister's wife. She couldn't play the piano. In fact, she didn't even sing. Couldn't carry a tune. No musical talent. Nada. Zero. And the couple only had one kid—a daughter.

But of course, it all worked out very well. The Reverend Addison proved to be a wonderful leader whose sermons drew many people into the church, for he possessed a formidable intellect and was a persuasive speaker with the power to move people. He was also found to have a remarkable dose of common sense and an aphoristic wit, and his good spirit and grace shone through in his relationships with all people.

And as the church rolls increased, the outreach mission of the congregation grew to more fully embrace the suburb and its hungry and destitute, which had long been unseen and ignored. Reverend Addison started a community pantry and filled it with food for the unemployed and homeless. He also began an alcohol and drug counseling center in the church basement.

He was also instrumental in working out a "sister church" arrangement with an inner-city congregation whose membership was almost entirely black. The two churches shared many activities, and he set up a swap between the two youth organizations in which the kids lived in one another's community for a week in the summer.

He did all this while becoming a marvelous spiritual leader of his congregation who was inspiring and compassionate, wise and kind. And he made everybody forget the Reverend Irene almost as soon as she departed.

A few members even found a certain poetry in the change of ministers when they discovered that the once-popular song "Goodnight Irene" had been written by a black man—the legendary Ledbelly.

Funny, He Doesn't Look Presbyterian

In a few years, the Reverend Addison became as beloved as Old Toplady. But perhaps his biggest influence on Christian life came in the presbytery.

When he was called to be the minister of the suburban congregation, he was the only minority pastor in a presbytery of forty-six churches. And he was often trotted out as a sort of example of white Christian tolerance. But his dignity, intelligence, and accomplishments gradually outgrew any consideration of race. In the eight years after his arrival, there were two Koreans, a Latino, and another black—a lady—called as ministers by the churches in the presbytery.

Everyone agreed that the fact that the Reverend Addison hadn't originally looked like the stereotypical Presbyterian was a blessing. And that his coming there was just another example of God's perfect good grace and timing in creating another small chapter in the Christian story.

About the Author

Bob Reed, a native of Marcus, Iowa, was raised a Methodist, married in the Congregational Church, and is now a member of the choir of the First Presbyterian Church of Northport (Long Island), New York, where he parties wildly all night-long with the church social group.

He plays the banjo and spent twenty-five years as an executive in public television and in college teaching, while writing things such as encyclopedias and dictionaries—all of which only partially explain this book. He also served in the Navy and is a proud grandfather. He is working on another book in this vein, currently titled *The Choir Who Couldn't Sing and Other Crazy Tales of Christian Life.*